SOMETIMES OUTNUMBERED.
NEVER OUTGUNNED.

It's zero hour on the English Channel. Europe's leaders are gathered to celebrate a historic event. And undetected by security forces, the world's most-feared assassin plans the ultimate terrorist coup.

The enemies of freedom play rough. But nobody plays rougher than the two-man strike force of Duggan and Dye . . .

CONFIRMED KILL

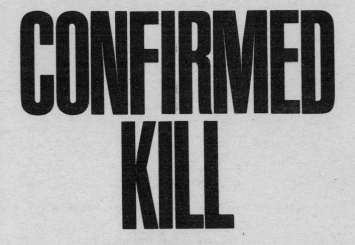

CONFIRMED KILL

MIKE MORRIS

DIAMOND BOOKS, NEW YORK

CONFIRMED KILL

A Diamond Book / published by arrangement with the author

PRINTING HISTORY
Diamond edition / March 1992

ISBN: 1-55773-581-6

Diamond Books are published by The Berkley Publishing Group,
200 Madison Avenue, New York, New York 10016.
The name ''DIAMOND'' and its logo are trademarks
belonging to Charter Communications, Inc.

PRINTED IN THE UNITED STATES OF AMERICA

10 9 8 7 6 5 4 3 2 1

MEMO

FROM: Office of Defense Intelligence Agency
DP-3
RM C760, Pentagon
Washington, DC 20340-5037
Tel: (202) 694-4921 (AUTOVON 224-4921)

TO: National Security Agency (NSA)
Central Security Service
Attn: 84
Rm. 24256, Pentagon
Washington, DC 20301-5000
Tel: (301) 688-6964
(AUTOVON) 235-6964

SUBJECT: Weapon System/Material Acquisition Test
Desert Site #3, July 18, 1992

COPIES: J.C.S. Service Staffs

Dear Michael:

Moses has struck his staff, the waters have parted, wonder-gun lives! I know you and the President have been very interested in these tests. I must stress here that the tests are preliminary, and technical adjustments will be an ongoing activity.

I'm not exactly sure what I saw. As you know, I'm a lawyer, not an engineering expert. The gun is not really a gun. It is a crew-served system, requiring maintenance and support and power packs carried in backpack-sized units.

It is called the SIKIM-1000 (See It, Kill It, Multiple Skill) weapon, nicknamed "Sikum!"

The weapon has lasint capability (as you know lasint means laser intelligence).

A.   It is a laser-guided weapon; a weapon that utilizes a "seeker" to direct laser energy reflected from a laser marked/designated target and through signal processing (M.—read here, computer!) provides guidance commands to a control system (computer!) which guides the weapon to the point from which the laser energy is being reflected.

B.   It has a built-in laser scan device.

C.   It "reads" its target! Height, weight, movement. Translates heat energy into visual scope display (VSD). "Target down" information confirmable.

D.   The weapon has four (4) projectile systems, using four (4) interchangeable launch tubes (barrels). It employs 1) high velocity, standard Columbia-system sniper ammo in .30 caliber, to 1000 yards; 2) explosive .40 caliber rounds to 1500 yards; 3) anti-material .50 caliber round to 3000 yards; 4) energy depletion (kill) round of pure heat, which has a 60% failure rate at this time. It was 1 for 3 in the demonstration. I watched a moving antelope, traveling at 40 mph and 2500 yards away just sort of blow up!

The guy that built this thing is a really weird member of our agency. The weapon is beyond belief, I must say. I saw it do things with my own eyes that I would never have believed otherwise. SIKIM-1000 is the ultimate shoulder weapon, probably into the 21st century. But, if it is to be efficient, we need a steady "shooter" type to make it so. Video cassette your office on Wednesday. I hope you get your man. Please give my regards to the President.

                                    Paul
Technical data sheet enroute.

Kenai, Alaska
September 30, 1992

The bear ambled along the ridge, fat with a summer's plunder of berries and fish and the bounty that Alaska supplies its wildlife in the short but spectacular months before the harsh winter season.

Con Duggan settled his binoculars on the bear, then, with the careful "check-it-out" attitude he seemed to have been born with, he glassed in the area around the bear. Michael Barns, his hunting companion, settled down and began to track the brownie with his rifle scope, the barrel of the gun resting across a rock.

"Not that one, Mike. Up on the ridge. Just this side. Big fucker coming down real careful."

"Where? I don't see him."

"He's not moving now. Just wait. He'll be along."

"How far up? I can't find him."

"Nine hundred yards. Maybe less. Maybe more."

"Hell, Con, why don't you take him?"

1

Con Duggan looked at his old friend, smiled, and spit his cigarette out of his mouth. He sat straight down, slung the .300 magnum and locked it into his shoulder. Michael Barns watched carefully.

The rifle shifted, looking small in the ex-Marine's hands. His massive shoulder curled around the weapon. You couldn't tell where the man ended and the weapon began. The barrel moved slowly, as if it were sniffing the wind.

The safety clicked off a split second before the gun roared out in anger, powder flashing briefly in the late afternoon gloom. The barrel jumped, but that was the only apparent recoil effect on Con Duggan.

Nine hundred seventy five yards away, the twelve-hundred-pound bear jumped straight up in the air, then began to roll down the hill, a brown, furry bowling ball knocking down stunted trees and bushes, ripping a two-hundred-yard trail before coming to rest against a dead white, thousand-year-old snag.

Michael Barns looked at Con Duggan with appreciation and not a little touch of awe. "Boy, you still have it, don't you." It was not a question, but a statement.

"What's that, Mike? What do I still have?" Michael Barns, Deputy Director of the CIA, just slung his unfired rifle over his shoulder and grinned at Con Duggan.

"Balls, I hope. C'mon, let's go look at that bar!"

Waiting for CIA agent Barns to say what had brought him to Alaska, aside from the transparent cover of a bear hunt, Con Duggan led the way across the valley to his "bar."

Com Pein, Cambodia
September 30, 1972

Marine Master Sergeant Conrad (Con) Duggan had been watching the "hooch" tucked back into the dank, steamy Cambodian jungle for over three days. He had finally decided that May-Lin Theu was, in fact, in the hooch, with two other NVA officers. Of course, the hooch itself was empty. The thatch roof and walls served only to conceal the network of underground tunnels that honeycombed the area.

From his place of concealment, the hooch was on a line with his position across a deep, lush valley. Nearly a thousand yards, he knew. Far enough to escape. Close enough to kill. He had removed the silencer because he needed the extra foot-per-second it would give him. Muzzle velocity at this distance would be hard to spare.

He had seen her once in Saigon, walking along the street in a western, but slightly Chinese-looking dress, slit to the thigh on both sides. She was very tall for a Vietnamese, almost five feet ten inches. She had a lithe, fragile-looking body. Black hair braided and hanging to her waist. The station chief had given him a wry, man-to-man wink. He tried to imagine her in bed, but he couldn't get past the image of her hunched over a Soviet-made sniper rifle, killing CIA field operatives and Marine commanders from one end of Vietnam to the other. It was hard to have erotic thoughts about a woman you had been ordered to kill. She was the daughter of a high-ranking provincial governor. Saigon had not been the place to terminate her.

But he was in the right place now. He was sure she would show up. Right here. Right in the doorway of that hooch that wasn't a hooch. His bones ached. She would be number one hundred. Jesus. One hundred human beings. It was duty. It was country. But goddamn, it was plenty tough to deal with.

Alaska, 1992

"Nice bear, Con. A real nice bear!"

"Yup. A nice one. Now, Michael, get down here and help me skin the SOB. What do you think you are, a fucking tourist?"

"Yeah, in a way I am. I'm here to tour your mind."

"Bad choice, Michael. Nothing in my mind except women and wilderness."

"How is Maggie, by the way?" There was a sly tone to the CIA man's voice.

Con Duggan slipped the cape knife around the bear's skull, working very efficiently. He didn't look up, just went about the business of skinning and quartering the huge animal he'd killed with one shot to the heart from nine hundred plus yards away.

"She's fine. Wants to get married and move to the lowland. Seattle, most likely. She wants me to buy her a boat."

"Domesticity. My, my. Con Duggan—married! Hard to imagine." Michael Barns smiled broadly as his needling tone brought Duggan up short.

"*She* wants to get married. Not me. I'll too old for babies. Hell, I'm too old for goddamn near everything."

"Do you know why I'm up here, Con?"

"I think so. I figure you'll tell me, but not until I do all the work with this terrific son-of-a-bitch bear I shot for you to brag about."

"Old Con. Good old Con."

"True. Now what do you want, Michael?"

"Okay. I guess I owe you a straight answer, considering I came up here to beg. We're forming a unit. A very special unit. We want you to come back, Con."

"You're out of your fucking mind!" All the light had drained away from Con Duggan's face. He stood up, glaring at Michael, his hands red with the blood of his kill. He looked carved from granite. His eyes were dark, gray-flecked fires, dancing in anger. Michael Barns and the CIA had better walk very carefully.

Cambodia, 1972

Con shifted his weight as best he could and sort of squatted, doing tiny knee bends that kept his head down in the sawtooth grass. He knew he was right. She was going to walk out of that "mirage." And, if she did, he was going to . . .

And then she was there. Like a wood sprite sprung

from the earth, a trick worthy of Merlin. He scrambled into shooting position, pulling the old reliable 1903 Springfield to his shoulder, the scope settling on the hooch doorway and she was . . . gone. Back inside. Lost to him. A kill denied. He felt like an outrun tiger, the sleek impala buck jumping out of the way. But she was there. He would wait. Waiting is what he did best. His muscles quit hurting. He was in the right place. She would be back. And he would kill her.

Alaska, 1992

The two men struggled to pull the cheesecloth over the quarter sections of the brownie as the Alaskan night clamped down on them suddenly, in the way unique to Kenai.

"We have this kid."

"Who? Who is we? Who is 'this kid'?" Con's voice was hard and raspy, a combination of physical exertion and complex emotional conflict.

"The agency. We. Me. Hell, Con, you know how it works! We have this kid, and he's developed this . . . this . . . gun. This weapon. And he wants to be our shooter."

"Fine. Let him be. Get me some more of that cheese-cloth before we lose all our daylight."

"He's a kid. Talented, but a kid. You know the type, Con. Hell, you *were* the type."

"I was never the type, Michael. Not ever."

"Yeah. Yes you were. You're the best, and this new unit needs the best. That's why I'm here."

"I'm psycho, Mike, remember? I'm retired because you people retired me. You got a good shooter, with a super-gun? Fine. You got no problems."

"We have new, unprecedented charter change here, Con. This unit is cleared to hit the bad guys. By Presidential order."

"The President has altered the charter?"

"He has."

"How?"

"We are free to attack our enemies—by whatever means—anywhere in the world."

"Even in the United States?"

"Yes."

"Money?"

"Unlimited."

"Assets?"

"Unlimited."

"Support?"

"Unlimited."

"What's the catch?"

"We need you to make it all work."

"That's bullshit, Mike, and you know it. Pass the cloth, will yah?"

Cambodia, 1972

Night in Southeast Asia descended very much like a quickly drawn window shade. Light simply went away, top to bottom, suddenly. Con Duggan was about to settle in for his fourth night of waiting. He ran a cloth patch through the already spotless barrel of his '03, a habit continued to insure success, like wearing the same shirt during a coaching win streak.

Master Sergeant Duggan was a superstitious man, and he was trying to cut the "white rabbit" odds against him. Ninety-nine kills. The gap between ninety-nine and one hundred seemed very long indeed. What did it mean, exactly? One hundred kills. Fuck it. He was a shooter, not a shrink.

He took what he thought would be his last look through the rifle scope before total darkness fell. The scope was full of NVA officers, including the most dangerous woman in the North Vietnamese arsenal. In less time than it takes to think, he centered the Springfield's scope on her and pulled the trigger.

He would never forget the video clarity of the next split-second. The small, black-clad child leaping upward, into her arms, the terrible wrath of the 180 grain Colum-

bia arms ammo ripping into and through her small, narrow body, knocking her mother backward, dead before she crashed into the hooch wall, her daughter clutched to her chest, also dead.

He chambered another round, fired, chambered, fired. Repeated the process five times until the star-clad uniforms and the small, crumpled body of the child blocked and sealed the hooch doorway. Number one hundred confirmed. He leaned forward over the weapon, his heart hammering inside his fatigues. This time he knew he would have to see his work. Up close. He hurried across the canyon, oblivious to the branches that crashed against his face, oblivious to the tears. A kid. A little kid . . .

The two men sat close to the campfire, the work with the bear finished, the liver cooking in its onion-filled pan, chopped bacon added, macho men with a macho meal.

"Tell me, Michael, why would you want me? I spent fucking near two years in the reverse straight jacket ward. You know that."

"Yes, I do. I visited you over twenty times."

"Through the one-way glass."

"True."

"And I've been here in Alaska for eighteen years, clean with the Game Department."

"A better ranger they've never had, I'm sure."

"I'm the best, no doubt."

"We want you to come back because you're the best at everything you do. We have a lot of hot-headed kids, hot shots, computer nerds, congressional intelligence appointees. You know the bunch."

"No. I stayed away from that bunch!"

"Fine. I'll keep you free from them. No strings. If you say its no go . . . we don't go."

Con stirred the dark mass of bear kill and condiments, savoring the wild smell, the sizzling, crackling meat of his long-shot kill a kind of music. For eighteen years, he'd hidden himself in the wilds of Alaska. Game agent, guide, hunter. Now, the crazy quilt of politics had sought him out.

As he dished up Michael's eagerly offered plate, he decided. "Tell me what I can do, Michael. I'll listen."

Cambodia, 1972

The hike had taken him over four hours. He'd not been careful, or it would have taken him eight. A bright moon lit the clearing around the hooch. He didn't hesitate. He walked directly to the woman, still clutching the fragile tiny body of her seven-year-old daughter. He knew it was her daughter.

There was a small, neat hole in the girl's back. She looked like she was asleep. The Columbia 180 grain bullet had been tracking at 2400 feet per second when it struck her. It tore through her back, exited just below her breastbone, and thundered into her mother. The only woman ever awarded North Vietnam's highest decoration for heroism would not kill again. Her eyes were open, staring upward, her arms crablike around her daughter's thin shoulders. It was here that Con Duggan, master sergeant, United States Marine Corps, stepped over the line between the living and those who have lived too much, too long, or too harshly.

Without expression, he began to drag the male officers killed by his sudden, terrible ambush into the hooch. He lined them up, noting in some small, distant part of his mind that all four of them were colonels.

He stared down at the mother and child, his eyes vacant, expressionless. Gently, he picked the tiny girl from her mother's breast, registering only briefly the large hole in the NVA sniper's chest. He carried the girl into the hooch, returned for her mother, and placed her next to her daughter. He closed her eyes with his fingers, but they flew open, accusing him.

He left the hooch, flicked his Zippo, and watched it burn to the ground, sitting cross-legged before the hut until nothing stood above ground. Four men, one woman, and a child.

A hunting chopper on a free-kill flight picked him up ten days later in the parrot's beak section of Cambodia. His insertion team had long since given him up for dead. All things considered, it was a sound move . . .

Con Duggan and the deputy director of the CIA had spent four days in the Alaskan wilderness, exorcising old ghosts and reforging old, strong ties. They had served together in multiple situations for six years in Southeast Asia. They liked each other. They trusted each other. Finally, they agreed to agree.

Chapple Lake, Alaska

The bright red Otter seaplane circled the lake once before Con dropped abruptly toward the smooth surface of the water. Michael was not comfortable in small planes, and Con Duggan knew it. He flew the Otter like an airborne "dodgg-em" car at an amusement park. The CIA man looked plenty green as they settled onto the lake, taxiing directly to the dock below Con's cabin. A wisp of white smoke spiralled into the crisp, blue sky, and Maggie Stuart, of the Boston Stuarts, waved from the open doorway.

As Con secured the Otter, Michael returned Maggie's wave. "She looks mighty fine, Con. Why a woman like that would take up with a man like you never ceases to amaze me."

Con only grunted. It amazed him too. Maggie Stuart came from blue-blood stock, Boston bred and educated. But she had been with Con Duggan for over fifteen years. Con never talked about how they wound up sharing a hand-built cabin in the far north, and you could believe any one of fifty tall tales about it. No matter. They were well matched.

"Hello, Michael. You're looking well." Maggie took the agent's heavy coat, hanging it on a wooden peg in the cheerful, bright kitchen. Four trays of freshly baked cookies cooled on a wooden chopping block.

The cabin was rustic but well equipped. A great deal of loving care had gone into its construction. It was two stories and very large. Nobody else lived on Chapple Lake. A radio telephone connected them to the outside world. And, of course, they had the Otter. Con Duggan, in his typically thoughtful, conservative way, had learned to fly before he came to Alaska.

Maggie busied herself with cookies after making the two men fresh coffee. Michael studied her as she moved about the room. Long black hair, with a startling streak of white about two inches wide running down one side from above her right eye. The hair reached below her slim waist, blanketing wide, sensual hips. She had very long legs, sleekly evident even through her jeans. She wore heavy wool socks and a red-and-black-checked wool shirt, the top two buttons open. She had heavy, full breasts, and they swung easily with her movements. She had a ruddy, Irish complexion, augmented by many hours spent outdoors. Her mouth was generous and inviting, her eyes a deep, arctic blue. Michael thought she was one of the most naturally beautiful women he'd ever seen.

"What brings you up here to God's country, Michael? We haven't seen you in . . . five years, isn't it?"

"Six, Maggie. Too long away from you, Mags. You're more beautiful than ever."

"Snake oil, I say!" But she blushed with pleasure when she said it.

"I just needed some great outdoors, that's all. Con shot me a bear."

"You're supposed to shoot your own, Michael."

"True. But I never could shoot, you know that. Even back in 'Nam,' I could spot and all, but I never could shoot."

Maggie skipped past the Vietnam reference. "How are things in the hallowed corridors of power, Michael? Are you running everything yet?"

"Yup. Most everything, anyhow. I saw your dad the other day."

"Oh? How does he look?"

"Like a senator. He looks like all senators."

"I haven't spoken to him since his last election. He sort of disowned me. Thinks I'm wasting my life up here with Con."

"He's right." Con Duggan sipped his coffee, looking at Maggie over the cup rim.

"No, he's not. I'll not have you saying that." She walked to his side, and kissed his nose, handing him a cookie in the process.

"Plying you with cookies, huh, Con. Boy I've seen everything now." But Michael's voice showed he was green with envy.

Maggie's back arched above him, her head thrown back, her black hair swinging across his legs as she climaxed. She held him inside her, her strong thighs gripping him, until her breathing slowed to normal and she rolled to her side, one sleek leg thrown across him as a rush of cool air momentarily chilled him. He pulled the comforter over their bodies, and she idly stroked his thigh with her fingertips, her breast heavy and warm against his chest. A customary ending to their usual lovemaking. But she sensed a difference.

"You're leaving, aren't you, Con?"

"Yes. I was going to tell you. Michael's going back to D.C. tomorrow. I'm supposed to meet him in Seattle on the 12th."

"Why?"

"Because he said it was important."

"What? What is so important you could leave me?"

"I'm not leaving you, Maggie. I'm going stateside for a while. I'll be back in a couple of weeks. Michael is the only man in the world I'd do this for. He asked me to help him. I figure I have to."

"Would it do any good to ask you to stay?"

"Don't do that to me, Maggie. Don't put me in that kind of spot."

"Okay." She pulled away from Con, her back to him. He let it go. She was just proving she could leave him, too.

Seattle, Washington
October 12, 1992

"Con Duggan, I'd like you to meet Steven Dye. He built and developed a weapon you won't believe."

Steven Dye was whip-thin, with unfashionably long reddish hair. He wore a black leather jacket, black leather pants, and a black turtleneck. All very dramatic. All very pretentious. All leaving a bad taste in Con Duggan's mouth. And it showed. Immediately.

"So, you're a wonder-gun."

"Sir?"

"Oh, shit, Michael . . . Sir?" Con gave Michael a disgusted look.

"C'mon, Duggan, give the kid a break."

"Okay. But this is hardly my idea of a match made in heaven."

Seattle-Tacoma International Airport
October 12, 1992

The three men sat in one of the sprawling airport's

13

lounges. Michael watched Con Duggan and Steven Dye very carefully. The two men couldn't have been more different. Yet, somehow, they had to mix well. It didn't look too promising to the Deputy Director of the CIA.

"I'm not saying Vietnam wasn't an honorable fight, Mr. . . . Duggan, for guys like you that were there. I'm just saying it was a bad war, at the wrong time."

"I see. And what, in your opinion, is a good war, at a good time?"

"Discernible evil."

"I beg your pardon?"

"Mr. . . . Duggan, we were in Vietnam for our own interests, not the Vietnamese. There was no discernible evil until we got there."

"How old are you, kid?"

"I was born in 1968."

Con Duggan got up abruptly and walked out of the lounge. Michael caught up with him, but it took stern words to get him back.

By one A.M., the lounge had quieted, and the drinks had relaxed the tension between Con Duggan and Steven Dye considerably. And Michael had begun to point out why they had been asked to form the backbone of a unit unique to American policy. Legal hit men, formed to promote freedom through the abrupt termination of enemies of the United States and the free world.

"Now listen to me, Con and Steven. You two must be able to work together. We have put together a lot of money, a lot of hardware, and a massive amount of intelligence data. This unit, this *strike* unit, can and will be a viable force against terrorists, drug dealers and dictators all over the world. But it needs good people. The best people! Con, you're the best sniper the Marines have ever produced. Your courage and resourcefulness are without equal. You're an experienced shooter with command experience. Steven, you're the future of this unit. You're a fine shot, a terrific weapons man and designer, but you have no experience. You've only been with the agency for two years. And you've never fired a weapon in anger.

Con will be the unit leader, and that's it. I don't want either of you to enter into a contract with the agency if these arrangements seem to be insurmountable. You can walk away, right now. But if you're in, you're in."

Steven Dye looked across the table at the massive form of Con Duggan. Could he work with this guy? Steven Dye was half Con Duggan's age. He was an erratic genius, a master's degree in engineering in hand at the age of twenty. He was a martial arts expert with a tendency to kick ass at the drop of a pair of panties. He was erratic and as volatile as his red hair might indicate. He was also brilliant, a crack shot, fearless about everything but spiders, and a patriot of unquestionable value. Most people believed he would one day head the agency, if not the country. His main sin was youth, and unfortunately, it was a sin that only time would forgive.

"I'm in," said Steven Dye.

"So am I," said Con Duggan.

"Good. In the morning we'll head to Nevada. It's about time I showed you your toys. See you in the A.M. Stay out of trouble, okay?"

Con Duggan looked at Steven Dye, and grinned. They wouldn't get into any trouble. Not tonight. But someday soon, all hell would likely break loose.

Hangar 21A, Nellis Air Force Base Nevada

The black-painted C-130, in spite of its bulk, seemed small in the vast spaces of newly built hangar 21A, set off by itself and adjacent by taxiway to the airstrips of the Tactical Fighter Weapons Center.

"Is that thing ours?" Con Duggan walked toward the sinister-looking transport plane. He noticed it was without markings of any kind.

"Yeah, it's ours. Sort of our own little truck. We have whatever decals we need for it, depending on where we might be going."

"Do you know where that is, Michael?"

"Yeah. We have three missions in planning."

"You *will* tell us about it, won't you?" asked Steven Dye, trailing his hand along the wheel carriage of the C-130.

"Soon. Climb in and check it out."

The C-130 for their as-yet unnamed unit was equipped with electronic gear for nearly every imaginable occasion. It was armed with Vietnam-era mini-guns and equipped to sleep twelve agents if required. The cargo area held two jeep-like vehicles in desert colors. From a cursory examination, Con Duggan decided it was a very sophisticated aircraft indeed.

"Can you fly this, Duggan?"

"If I had to, Steven. But only if I had to. Hopefully, a pilot comes with it."

The three men sat down in the comfortable, high-backed seats along one wall of the aircraft, around a table covered with a fitted plexiglas top. It was a photo/light table with double usage as a place to put your can of beer. Nice touch, thought Con. Somebody had spent a lot of time, possibly years, putting this new show together. He was feeling better all the time.

"This hangar has a completely operational communications and satellite unit, capable of keeping in touch with you throughout the known universe. You'll often be alone, but we'll be listening."

"Some comfort," mused Con.

"Yeah. But just some." Steven Dye liked Con Duggan. And he was surprised at that. Con grinned at him. A hangman's grin.

"There are enough explosives and weapons in this hangar to start a revolution. We'll train constantly out in the desert until you can use them all. Of course, your main, and most useful, weapons will continue to be those designed for termination in silence at long distances. You are, after all, snipers." Michael looked at both men, one older, graying, a saddened but wise veteran. A true shooter. And the younger man, thin, intense, a little bit fanatic. What he had here, he thought, was a two-headed killer of considerable skill. Alone they were impressive. Combined, they were nearly unbeatable. The world's bad guys were in for a world of hurt. . . .

"Well, Con, what do you think?" Michael Barns had a smile on his face and glee in his voice. He'd expected this dark hangar corner to be his "ace," if Con Duggan had balked. Con had not balked, so this corner of Hangar 21A was now a happy gift, not an inducement.

"Holy shit!" Con let his breath expel in surprise, his eyes widening, a look of pure astonishment transforming his face from his normal granite countenance to boyish excitement.

Two spotlights shone down from the arched ceiling of the hangar roof like show lights on a chorus girl in Las Vegas, just down the highway from Hangar 21A. But to Con Duggan, no chorus girl had finer lines than he saw before him.

"Where did you get it, Michael?"

"Oh, here and there. It's about 70% original. We sort of manufactured the rest of it."

"It" was a 1942 version of the twin-engined WWII British "Mosquito" fighter bomber, one of the fastest, most effective ground-attack aircraft ever built. It was made of wood, and therefore, radar evasive. It could bring a great deal of firepower onto a target at nearly 450 mph, flying at the attack height of fifty feet. There were fewer than a half-dozen Mosquitoes in the world still flyable.

"It has been modified a bit, Con. She's got the same Rolls Royce engines, but a lot faster, about 550, we think. You'll have to fly her and see. The gun pods can hold more modern weaponry, including Mr. Dye's "Wonder Gun," but it still is basically a hot, flyable aircraft over 50 years old. We felt—we knew, actually—that you'd like it a lot."

"You mean like a bribe?"

"Yeah. Sort of a bribe. But you get it anyway. Your name is on the forward fuselage."

"Sure of yourself, huh, Michael?"

"No. Not sure. But I should have been." Michael gave Con Duggan a disarmingly innocent smile.

"When can I fly her?"

"Tomorrow. Tomorrow, we talk mission, and we start to find out if our equipment works."

"You mean you don't know yet?"

"Well . . . in theory we know. You and Steven will prove it all out, of course."

"Terrific. Just terrific . . ."

"Isn't it? I knew you'd enjoy trying all the new toys yourself."

"Michael, you should have been a car salesman. Or maybe real estate."

"I was. Both. Long ago." Michael Barns, the possessor of magnificent toys and permission to give them away, walked out of Hangar 21A and into the night, leaving Con Duggan with his Mosquito, and his private thoughts.

Con sat in the Mosquito cockpit shifting his weight, trying to get comfortable in the pilot seat, its back hard and unyielding against his. The instrument panel was simple and uncluttered. How fast, how high, how much gas left, the basic information a pilot needed to survive fifty years ago. Con Duggan had been six years old in 1942. He remembered the old newsreels toward the war's end, the Mosquitoes racing along the ground, shooting up trains, flack towers, trucks, and just anything at all that moved in Germany. Now, he would fly one. He shifted again. The seat would have to go. If he were going to fly this old warbird, his old back would need better support than the hard aluminum seat provided.

The plane rocked a bit as Steven Dye climbed onto the wing and folded his lanky body next to the open cockpit. "Will this thing actually fly?"

Con gave Steven Dye a pained look and a curt reply. "Yeah, it will fly. I'm going to take it up in the morning. You're going with me."

Alarm spread across Steven Dye's handsome, angular face. His red hair seemed to get redder.

"Oh, no I'm not. I like airliners. 747s. You want to play with this, you go ahead. Me, I'll stay down on the ground."

"Someday, we may use that gun of yours I've heard so little about. In this plane. And you'll *have* to fly with me then. Might as well start now. Hell, you might like it, Steven."

"Not likely, Mr. Duggan. How old is this crate?"

Con decided that Steven Dye was not only young, he was a pain in the ass, too.

"Fifty years. It was built originally in 1942, just as it sits here. But it's been souped up a little. But basically it's a fifty-year-old airplane."

"Jesus! Fifty! That's an old plane."

"I'm fifty-five, Steven, so we sorta fit, don't you think?"

"Well, Con . . . Mr. Duggan, I didn't mean anything by that. I just meant—"

"I know what you meant, Steven. Yes, it's an old airplane. And I'm an old shooter. But we, the plane and I, are not yet ready to retire. Now, if you want to rest up for our flight in the morning, I suggest you hit the sack."

"But, but, I'm not going up in this—"

"Yes, Mr. Dye! You are! Tomorrow! Now go away, and leave us old folks alone."

Steven Dye was going to say something smartassed, which was his usual way of dealing with people. Something in Con Duggan's eyes constricted his vocal cords just in time. He hopped off the Mosquito's wing and did as he was told. He went to bed, leaving the two old "shooters" alone in the vast, semi-darkened Hangar 21A. Home base for an operational group of spies and counterspies that couldn't have been more mismatched in his view. But Steven Dye was very young. And he was wrong. It was actually a match made in spy heaven.

• • •

An F-117A Stealth fighter taxied along the Nellis Air Force Base north runway. A new X-Series tactical fighter was right behind it, the new fighters still engaged in a flyoff with the General Dynamics/McDonald prototype being ministered to on the south flight line. Nellis was a very busy base, with over 200 aircraft on the ground at any one time. The tower was controlled pandemonium, sending operational and test flights off and retrieving earlier flights with nimble efficiency.

"Tower, this is Mosquito 21A requesting permission to taxi East Strip, 21A Hangar taxiway."

The air-traffic controller pulled his binoculars to his face, stared for a moment, and regained his speech processes.

"Holy shit! I mean . . . I mean, roger, Mosquito 21A, permission to taxi East Strip. Your runway station behind tac fighter on North Strip. Uh, 21A, are you going to fly that thing?"

"That's a roger, tower. 21A out."

"Jesus Christ!" said the flight controller. The six men and two women in the tower fixed their binoculars on the black-painted apparition. Ahead of it, the angular odd-shaped tactical fighter of the future moved briskly to its take-off space. Five hundred yards and 50 years of flight technology separated them.

The number one engine of the Mosquito fired smoothly, belching a cloud of quickly dissipating black smoke and, to Steven Dye's unpracticed eye, an engine fire as well. Con Duggan smoothed the port engine out and fired the number two engine on the starboard wing. To Steven Dye, this engine-start was even worse than the first one. Two engines. Smoke. Fire. Holy shit!

"Now, let me see here," said Con Duggan. "This must be the rudder pedal, and this, this must be the brake. Now just where the hell is the "go" button? Mr. Dye, do you see the throttle in this pathetic old crate?" Steven Dye, pale complexioned to begin with, turned a sickly white face toward Con Duggan. Con was looking at him, a nasty, not quite perverted smile on his face. "Oh, my God, I'm doomed," said Steven Dye.

"That's okay, kid. I know where the go button is. Of course, we're only in the taxi mode right now. Damned if I can figure out how to get this sucker into the air."

Con Duggan kicked the Mosquito loose and moved slowly down the 21A taxiway toward the north runway. Ahead of him, the ominous-looking prototype of the United States's latest and probably final tactical fighter strained at its brakes, jet engines screaming into the dry desert air, a massive but startlingly quick twenty-first century answer to air-to-air combat. Behind it, dwarf-size in comparison, the Mosquito bobbed like an ungainly insect on its awkward, 1940's undercarriage. Suddenly, the tactical fighter, an instant after it had clearance from the tower, leapt down the long runway and into the air in a near-vertical climb, vanishing into the arid blue in seconds.

Con Duggan rolled the tiny Mosquito into position and looked down the 12,000-foot runway. He would need about 1000 of those feet.

"21A."

"21A," replied the tower.

"Permission to fly, tower."

"Hell, 21A, if it will fly, you certainly have my permission."

"Roger, tower. Permission to fly 21A . . . out."

"21A." The tower man kept his glasses fixed on the apparition from another time.

"Well, Mr. Dye? Shall we?" Mr. Dye was too scared to look at Con Duggan. He gripped the sides of his seat, giving new and vivid meaning to a white-knuckle flight. The Mosquito vibrated violently. Steven Dye was afraid it might shake itself to pieces, the Rolls Royce Merlin engines straining all of their 1710 hp as Con Duggan let them run out to their taxiway. He kicked the fighter-bomber loose, and it lurched forward, picking up speed, going faster, it seemed, than Steven Dye had ever experienced. The Mosquito wasn't going *that* fast, but it was very small, very noisy, and it seemed to tip violently down to the left. Con Duggan righted the aircraft, and it was airborne, the ground rushing away in a blur as Steven Dye looked earthward, doubtful that he would ever walk its green grasses again.

Con Duggan flew the Mosquito northward into the desert, checking gauges, watching oil pressure, speed, altitude, engine temperature. The engines were noisy, but it was a loud purr of perfection. He tested the controls, weaving the aircraft in a slow "S" turn. It was responsive and true to its heritage. Skittish, but a fast lady with class. She was not really a lady, but, oh my. . . .

Steven Dye, much to his surprise, was having a pretty good time. The view was spectacular from 12,000 feet, and it was a beautiful day. He settled down, his pale knuckles less white, his composure returned.

"Hey, Con, this is a piece of cake." At that moment, the "piece of cake" went into a power dive headed straight for a deep canyon whose walls where less than 120 feet apart.

It would be six months before Steven Dye would trust himself to remember that flight into, through, and, thank God, out of the canyon in Nevada. He retained only pieces of it, a jigsaw puzzle that he couldn't quite reconstruct. The canyon walls, he remembered, were reddish brown; clay, he supposed. The canyon bottom, incongruously, held a swift-running stream, glacier blue, which, he recalled, splashed up against the bottom of the Mosquito as they followed its course. He wasn't a fisherman, but with a net or a pair of panty hose, he could have been, simply by leaning out the cockpit window and dragging them in the water. The rocks in the stream were round and white, like seashells. The rocks on the sides of the stream were large . . . very large. A mountain lion and her two cubs, too startled to run, drank in the cool darkness of the remote canyon. And then they were free, spiralling upward, the engines straining as they clawed their way to 25,000 feet. Con Duggan levelled the tiny fighter-bomber and flew it steady and sure, looking across the 18 inches between himself and Steven Dye, a psychological gap of truly monumental proportions.

"Well, Mr. Dye?" Con Duggan's hard flint eyes bore into Steven Dye's and read, or tried to read, his soul.

With a strangled croak, not at all his voice, Steven Dye said, "Well, I liked it. Could we, uh, do that again?" The plane banked left and roared earthward. Six times, they negotiated the narrow, two-mile-long canyon at over 325 mph. After the sixth pass, he flew straight back to Nellis, doing a victory roll over the control tower that sent its personnel scrambling for safety under their desks. He landed without incident and taxied off to Hangar 21A, the Mosquito shuddering in suppressed excitement as he throttled down and shut her off. Mike Barns was waiting for them.

"How'd it go?"

"Piece-o'-cake. Right, Steven?" There was no sign of a taunt in Con Duggan's voice.

"Yeah. Right. A piece-o'-cake." If Steven Dye possessed a sly grin, he used it, extended it, to Con Duggan.

"Did you bring that paint, Michael?"

"Yup." Michael Barnes handed Con Duggan a can of silver paint and a brush. In an hour, under PILOT, CON DUGGAN, USMC, he had painted NAVIGATOR/GUNNER, STEVEN DYE, USA. Then he walked away, leaving Steven Dye to ponder the vagaries of life while holding a wet paint brush dripping silver paint on his leather coat.

Con Duggan had spent very little time in the desert. He had no idea it could get so cold. The morning was bright, crisp, and 27 degrees. Four helicopters had ferried them 120 miles, deep into a corner of the desert usually reserved for bomb impacts, road runners, coyotes, and Hell's Angels' drug labs. It was, to put it simply, remote. Like the Amazon is remote. Aircraft flew over the area, used the area, and it had been a tank base in 1942. The wind blew most of the time, dry and hot and terrible. Lawrence of Arabia should have strolled across the range on a camel, a director screaming for more wind, more dust, more misery. Con watched Steven Dye in his leathers, hunched over two long boxes that he'd been told contained Steven Dye's dream. Wonder-gun. Con tried to spit, but it was too windy, too dry, and too cold.

Michael Barns was hovering at Con Duggan's elbow, whispering into his ear. "It works, most of the time. But he's not very confident about the EDR function. Energy Depletion Rounds make Star Wars technology look positively uninspired. When it works—and the success ratio is rising—it's an awesome weapon. You'll like it, Con."

"A 60–70% success rate, and I'll like it? C'mon, Michael, don't snow me. I understand the SIKIM-1000 is in R & D. Let's leave it at that. I promise not to laugh when that mountain across the valley falls down by mistake when the SIKIM takes a wrong turn."

"Funny, Con, very funny." Michael did not look amused.

"Well, I think it's funny."

"He flew with you, Con. Help him. Hell, he's a good kid."

"Okay. I'll keep an open mind."

The SIKIM was a gun, but in some configurations, it was hard to identify as one. Con had shot it in its shoulder mode in .30, .40 and .50 caliber. It looked and felt like an overweight, long-barrelled M40-A1 sniper rifle. Fine. He'd used the M40-A1 a few times. He didn't care for it, but it was a very effective weapon, tried, true, reliable. The SIKIM-1000 had sophisticated, interchangeable barrels, so it could shift from a simple rifle to an anti–personnel carrier bust'n cannon. The .40mm round was a real pisser. He had blown up a new Cadillac with it at 2500 yards. One shot. The 51B recoil system that went on and off like a glove was very impressive. Nobody knew or cared why they called it the 51B system. The massive scope had brought the Caddy optically within a few feet. He'd been able to count rivets on the molding.

It also shifted from light to dark, infrared, Alto-gray and heat-emanated. Something he'd never seen before.

He'd used the gun while Steven Dye had watched, occasionally switching settings on his mysterious backpack power unit to heighten Duggan's view of his targets. He'd been able to read and hit a moving jack rabbit in a 28-foot runway, and the rabbit had been racing from one end of the runway to the other during the whole sighting process. One .30 caliber explosive round from 1500 yards. Duggan was the best shooter in the world. The sighting system in Steven Dye's backpack computer, tuned to the SIKIM-1000, made him good enough to shoot competitively for Mars in the next century. He was impressed. When the SIKIM was switched to Steven Dye's Energy Depletion Mode, handled by Steven Dye, he was flabbergasted, confused, scared, and most important to Michael, impressed and eager to see what it might one day produce.

Con Duggan was a shooter, deep down. The SIKIM was, or could be, an undefeatable shooter's aid in the right hands. Steven Dye's hands.

"If there's one major flaw to the SIKIM termination system, it is the bulk and weight of the sight/computer scope and backpack." Steven Dye was delivering a shirt-sleeve lecture about his wonderful gun. "The Energy Depletion Round as well as the Thermal Acceleration Device, which we call TAD, can actually use up the power available from the computer backpack after only one shot. I'm working on that problem, but sometimes I attempt to shoot the SIKIM, and it's like a car that won't start. We are talking pure energy as a launch/fire method—too complex to explain—but as I said, I'm trying to make the whole thing simpler. Down the road, it will be. For now, the success rate of the EDR and TAD is 50–70% at best. But it always works once in each mode every time the system is activated. So, the first two applications have a 100% success record. If I do the job right the first time, we are okay."

He cast a challenging glance toward Con Duggan, but got no reaction. Con just puffed on his cigarette, a faded

Marine Corps cap nearly hiding his craggy face from view.

"The exact maximum range of the EDR and TAD rounds is, quite frankly, still a mystery to me. I know how that sounds to you, Con, but the system is quirky, unpredictable, and most of the time unstable."

"Sounds like you, Mr. Dye." Con Duggan's remark provoked group laughter and loosened everybody up, particularly Steven Dye.

"True. Very true." Steven Dye's shoulders slumped as his tension evaporated. It would be okay, he thought.

"The Energy Depletion Round kills in a very unique and quite horrible way," Dye continued. "It withdraws energy of any kind within 20 inches of the target, causing the target to . . . to explode. Much like giving the target a bad case of the bends, putting it in a recovery chamber and pulling the plug at a time to, as I've stated, blow up the subject. The EDR deprives the target of an environment. Environmental deprivation in human beings creates an explosive vacuum. Essentially, that's how the EDR works." Steven Dye looked around at the small circle of men included in the Q/A support group unit. They did not seem to react negatively.

"How do you do this, Mr. Dye?" Con Duggan asked.

"With this." Steven Dye held up a slim black cylinder about 10 inches long. It had a blue tip and tiny red dots running from top to bottom. The base was yellow. It looked very much like an exotically painted dildo.

The antelope was loosely penned but constantly on the move, with over 1000 square yards to run in. Con Duggan had killed antelope long ago in Wyoming. You had to ship the meat by rail then, because the temperature in Wyoming during the late August/early September antelope hunt often approached one hundred degrees.

"Why an antelope, Mr. Dye?"

"Weight. Speed. Proof that the EDR can do some wondrous things. You've killed 100 men, Mr. Duggan. Does one antelope bother you?"

Con Duggan studied Steven Dye's face. Not smart-assed. Just a question.

"Actually, Mr. Dye, I've killed 101 men, one woman, and one female child. Cut the animal loose. Then shoot it—if you can." This time, there was real challenge in his voice.

"Another test, Mr. Duggan?"

"Why not, Mr. Dye? Life is a test, isn't it?"

Without a word to Con, Steven walked to the nearest Jeep and spoke into a radio. Within a minute, the "Net-Pen" came down. Steven Dye walked back to his station and sat down. He picked up the dildo-shaped EDR and inserted it into a flat magazine bolted to the side of the oversized M40-A1–styled sniper unit. He moved the bolt back and inserted a flat metal plate painted red on one side and yellow on the other. He jammed the bolt forward. A bright yellow band showed on the top of the receiver. It was lit from the bottom and pulsed like an automobile turn signal.

The antelope was at first startled by the dropped walls that had penned it in. The buck stood there, tense, its finely muscled body quivering like multiple guitar strings. The buck's nostrils flared, and it stamped its front feet, one, twice, three times.

The antelope jumped to one side, then another, then came to a standstill almost in the center of its now-nonconfining cage.

Con watched as Steven Dye moved a switch forward on the gun. The pulsing yellow square rolled over and into the gun's receiver, changing to a bright red, non-pulsing flow. The antelope seemed to fix his eyes on Steven Dye, an optical illusion heightened by distance. The weapon was 2000 yards from its target.

The antelope's tail went up, and it suddenly bounded away, racing northward at top speed, heading up a mountain in a zigzag pattern that increased both the distance from the shooter and the difficulty of the shot in split-seconds. The antelope was clearly going to get away.

A sharp, ear-shattering sound, like torn paper on a

monumental scale, accompanied by a bright blue flash in the gun's barrel shocked the watching team members into silence. A silence they would never forget.

Just before it crested the hill, the antelope vanished in a spray of blood and tissue. One moment it was straining to get away. The next, it was just gone. . . .

The men on the demonstration site were all experienced, qualified personnel in the "Black Arts" of espionage, counterespionage, terrorism, and all manner of dirty low-down tricks. But the virtual disappearance of a 125-pound animal moving at 40 miles an hour on an erratic path silenced them all. Well, not all.

"Nice shot, Stevo."

"Thanks, Con. You want to try?"

"I don't know, Mr. Dye. How fast can you run?"

The antelope had not, in fact, disappeared. Bits of bone and flesh, liberally sprinkled with blood, were now spread in a 100-yard circle where the antelope had been before Steven Dye's rectangle had gone from yellow to red. Con Duggan picked up a perfect set of antelope horns still attached to the skull bone, with the hair of the skull unsullied in spite of the bright sheen of blood sprayed neatly in a circular pattern on the side of the hill.

"A trophy, Con?" The questioner was Steven Dye.

"No, not exactly. But I thought we might mount it on the nose of the Mosquito. What do you think?"

"You're a very sick man, Mr. Duggan."

"That's true. But I didn't design the fucking evaporator from outer space, did I?"

Two days later, the Mosquito had a fine set of Western Antelope antlers mounted on its nose. It looked quite good, actually.

"The TAD round works a bit differently, gentlemen. What it does, in the simplest of terms, is apply thermonuclear heat to an area less than one foot by 6 inches. For a brief millisecond, the sun shines too bright, you might say."

"Example, Mr. Dye?"

"Okay. A hit on a window: no window, but no damage to anyone behind the window. A hit on a truck: melted steel and aluminum, but no pain to the interior."

"And to a human?"

"Barbecue, Mr. Duggan. You would melt if struck directly by the TAD round."

"Thermal Acceleration Device, correct?"

"Yes. Essentially, the TAD fries its target faster than you can blink your eyes. And I mean that. Faster than you can blink your eyes."

"But if fired against a blank wall of glass, it would only melt the glass? If I were standing, say, right behind the glass, I·would be unharmed?"

"Correct."

"Not too many uses for this round, eh, Mr. Dye?"

"I trust your ingenuity, Mr. Duggan. I'm sure you will find a use for the TAD."

"Why would you be sure of that, Steven?" The two men switched back and forth between formality and informality. Searching, like all good hunters.

"Because, Con, you have some cockamamie reputation as a very weird dude. I just naturally assumed you would find an application for the TAD."

"You are correct, Mr. Dye. I will find one. Now why don't you demonstrate how it works?"

Steven Dye looked down at his hands and shuffled his feet. "Well, truth told, I busted the power pack shooting the antelope."

"Mr. Dye?"

"Yes, Mr. Duggan?"

"You seem to be a fuck-up, sir."

"Well, part of the time, the system just doesn't work."

Con Duggan could think of nothing at all to say.

London, England
October 15, 1992

"Why don't we just blow it up?"

"Blow what up?" Booker knew what Dorsey was saying but did not acknowledge it.

"The bloody tunnel, that's what! Why do we have to shoot them?"

"Because they are paying us close to fourteen million pounds, Dorsey, now aren't they?"

"Well, it's not enough, if you ask me." Dorsey tossed back four water glasses of Scotch with no apparent effect.

"I didn't ask you, Dorsey." Booker's eyes narrowed with disapproval.

Dorsey Talbot McLean was Scotch-Irish by birth, and timid by nature. If you consider a man confident in the use of hand grenades, missile launchers, and the Bowie knife timid. He had personally sent over three hundred human beings to violent deaths, including a nice terrorist touch on a British Airways Boeing 767 with 247 vacationers on board. The largest single intact piece of the aircraft had been recovered by the United States Navy in '91 at a cost to the United States taxpayers of seven million dollars. The nine-feet-square piece of aluminum, a cross-section of the tail, had proven only that the aircraft had been blown up in flight by persons unknown.

Dorsey Talbot McLean carried a Baretta Model 92M 9mm semiautomatic, a four-inch knife in his boot, and a white phosphorous grenade in his baggy coat pocket. Nothing in the world could make his ferret-faced countenance show fear. Nothing, that is, except the man sitting across from him in the Lion's Mane pub, six Brixton Street, London, England, this day in October, 1992.

This man he feared. And so he should have. Peter Coy Booker, Australian-born, raised in Chicago, Illinois. Son of a prostitute notorious in the dark side streets of Sydney, not for her sexual favors, but for her nine illegitimate, fatherless sons. Peter Coy Booker, seven-time international combat pistol champion. Peter Coy Booker, owner of a house or villa on all the worlds oceans, as he put it. Peter Coy Booker . . . killer for hire. Killer for free. Killer . . . for the hell of it.

Peter Coy Booker, known simply as "Booker" to his acquaintances (he had no friends) was good looking, red-bearded and blue-eyed. A very dangerous man to know in view of the fact that many of the people he knew died before their times. He carried, as a matter of habit, a leather pouch full of the best cocaine money could buy. He spread it around among what he jeeringly called his "coke whores," young women with large breasts, long legs, and fried minds. Wherever he was, women flocked to him like docile sheep.

He used them, traded them, and gave them away. Many of them had died in the process. He did not use drugs himself. That would have diminished his capabilities, made him stupid, or dead. He was a compactly built machine, capable of feigned good humor and charm or massive, chaotic violence.

Booker looked at Dorsey across one of the polished

mahogany tables of the Lion's Mane, 150 years old, a pub still providing the citizens with a place to get stupid drunk. Dorsey was busy *getting* stupid drunk, a daily occurrence which he always managed to end when business had to be done.

"Tell me, Dorsey, just exactly how would you blow up the Chunnel, if you felt so obliged?"

Dorsey leaned back in the booth to allow the vacant-eyed blonde at his side ample room to thrust her sleekly painted fingers down the front of his pants. As always, Booker provided, yes he did. Dorsey shivered at her touch, both light and firm, one and the same. He concentrated on purging himself into her soft palm, in public, where he liked it best, because it was the only way Dorsey could achieve a climax. Well, not the only way. Lately, killing had worked just as well.

Dorsey said, "Well, it's underwater, isn't it? A fucking million tons of hydrostatic pressure. Find the bloody cork, and pull . . . pull it."

"So, Dorsey, you'd pull the plug? Do you even know where the bloody fucking plug is? No! You don't know, and we have one week. *One week*."

"That's enough. We did the Saudi king in six days." The blonde's ponytail was clenched in Dorsey's fist, while his other hand was thrust under her mini-skirt.

At the counter, the barmaid watched, eyes glittering, knowing, but paid hard cash not to know.

"Finish her, Dorsey, you bloody sot! Fuck her face, and get it over with! Then I'll tell you what we are going to do."

Booker got up, glancing down at the ponytailed, coked-out blond. He walked to the bar and blocked the woman's view.

"Forget it, darlin'. *She* will. How about a Scotch now?" Reluctantly, the barmaid paid the price for her silence by pouring the drink. She missed the action in the booth, which by that time had turned messy.

Hangar 21A, Nellis Air Force Base
Nevada
October 15, 1992

"I called you together for what I'm afraid will be an alarmingly short briefing. We have a problem to solve. I would have preferred more time, but this has come up, and I suggested we could do it."

Michael Barns snuffed out his cigarette and immediately lit another one. Con Duggan recognized the signs. Nervous, excited, committed to solving whatever "problem" he'd accepted for them.

"On October 21st, the Prime Minister of England and the President of France are going to take a ride together, from France to England, in the Chunnel, the tunnel just completed under the English Channel between those two countries. The idea, of course, is to show that it works, and is worth the forty billion dollars it cost. The Chunnel will not be open for public use until the finishing work is completed, supposedly by July of next year. But the tracks are down, and they have a ready train, so the politicians, as usual, will try to demonstrate why this idea is so useful, considering the bulk of the British public has opposed the idea from the outset. A train ride under the Channel by the two leaders will supposedly prove to that doubting public that the damn thing was worth the 40 billion.

"I'll skip the politics here. What we know is this. A plot to kill both of these worthies is underway. We have only seven days to stop it."

"Seven days. Well, Michael, do we know what it is we have to stop? I mean, do we know what the bad buys intend to do?" Con Duggan was not happy about this new unit's first, and maybe last, mission.

"No, actually we don't. I expect you and Mr. Dye to find that out."

Con glanced at Steven Dye, who gave a slight shrug of his shoulders and an arched eyebrow in response.

"Do we know who is going to perpetrate this shoot—or whatever this is?"

"Yes, Con. We do know who. Turn out the lights, and I'll show you a brief, grim little video." Shortly, Con Duggan's nightmares turned to grim reality. His chest tightened as he watched Michael Barns's horror show of bad guys.

"Lights, please."

The hangar briefing room lights went back on. Steven Dye looked ill.

"Did you recognize the man, Con?" asked Michael.

"Booker." Con Duggan spat the word like bad tobacco.

"Correct. Peter Coy Booker."

Steven Dye was not a timid soul, and he spoke right up. "You know this guy, Con? Jesus, I don't think I needed the closeup of the guys in that house. I mean, they were carved up! This guy Booker, he did that? Why the hell isn't he locked up instead of floating around the world in shooting competitions? Christ, you shot against this guy in the 1989 Steel Challenge Match! He was right next to you. Yachts, girls, guns, and dead bodies. Jesus!" Steven Dye had a comically incredulous look on his face. In spite of himself, Con could not suppress a grin.

"Well, Steven, I know it sounds weird. Booker, as you saw, is well-known worldwide. He's a freelance, non-political hit man, a suspect in dozens of cases. But just a suspect. I heard he did some time in an Italian jail in the 70's. But he bought his way out. Unfortunately, there are governments in the world that have need of Booker's . . . uh, talents. He's a certified crazy, with a few hundred millions in Swiss bank accounts. I had dinner with him way back in '72 in Cambodia. He can be very charming, as I recall."

"Jesus!" That exclamation was the best Steven Dye could offer at the moment.

London
Triangle Athletic Club
October 15, 1992

Booker whirled and kicked out, whirled again, struck quickly with both hands, sending his personal martial arts instructor into a defensive somersault away from Booker's lightning blows. At 45, Booker had a hard body and the reflexes of a man half his age.

The mixed-race Asian, well paid and a true master of the martial arts, moved forward, feinted to his left, and sent a tattoo of hard blows against Booker's chest. But not too hard. He knew better than to injure the goose that laid the golden eggs.

The two men fought on, the silence interrupted only by explosive bursts of combat, expelled air and grunts, the chorus to the main song of blows to exposed skin. It seemed stylistic and formal in spite of its violent intention. And it was. Style counted more than substance to Peter Coy Booker. He knew his trainer believed that Booker was not his martial arts equal. Someday Booker intended to show him just how wrong he was. Of course, he would have to actually kill him to prove it. With a final surprise onslaught, he blasted the Asian to his knees, bowed, and walked away. Something for his "Sensei" to think about.

Booker wiped his brow, wrapped a towel around his heavily muscled shoulders, and sat down on a straight-backed chair in the bare, mahogany-floored training room. Dorsey handed him a glass of water, and he drank it down. His body glistened with sweat. Booker wore only an oriental athletic supporter, not much more than string.

"I don't get what you see in this knocking one another about. Look at you. You'll have welts for days. I've been with you a long time, Booker, and I've yet to see you use that stuff."

"Well, Dorsey, one day I might use it. In the meantime, it keeps me in shape."

"Bugger shape! Look a' me, Booker. I'm fat and sloppy, but I can handle weapons now, can't I?"

Dorsey needed a compliment. Sitting next to his acknowledged leader, looking at Booker's near perfection, Dorsey had slipped into his usual, whiny ways. Booker ignored his henchman's need.

"I think, Dorsey, we should let the Prime Minister and the French President have their ride through the Chunnel, and then make the hit."

"And just how are we going to do that?" Denied his compliment, Dorsey grew pugnacious.

"I haven't quite decided. But I do know they will both helicopter back to their respective nests after the festivities at the English side of the Chunnel. I also know where they are going to helicopter from. There is a municipal sports ground in Folkstone, only a few minutes from the train's central station. It's large and flat, and that is where they will say goodbye."

"Oh? And 'ow in bloody 'ell do you know that?" Dorsey slipped back into his East End accent every five minutes, in spite of his efforts to get "cultured."

"Because I paid a tidy sum to a weak-willed British minister to find out." With a terribly swift move, Booker was out of his chair, his damp towel thrown over Dorsey's face, his fingers in a vise grip on Dorsey's throat. Speaking into the towel, he said, "Do you have any other doubts, Dorsey? I'm getting very tired of you. Mind you, Dorsey, very tired." With a casual flip, Booker tossed Dorsey ten feet across the polished floor to land in a crumpled heap against the white-painted walls.

Dorsey pulled the towel from his face only to see Booker's nearly naked body disappear through a doorway to the showers.

"Bloody 'ell. Oh, Jesus Mary. Bloody 'ell." He'd have to be more careful. Booker, after all, could kill him anytime with his bare hands. Not a man to fool with. No, not at all . . .

Chicago, Illinois
December 9, 1967

"Now, Petey, do you know what you're supposed to do here? I mean, kid, this guy, this guy you're gonna hit for us, he might not be alone up there in that room. We don't know. But Salvatore says you got balls, so I said, sure, why not, although I never used a non-made guy, ya know?"

"Petey" Booker kept quiet, but nodded his head. The man from the Cicero family, this hulking Italian who had just given him $2,000 in crisp hundred-dollar bills, this *"guy"* had nothing to worry about. Petey had killed his first man in Sydney, Australia, at the age of twelve. A pimp had been beating his mother and was taking her money from her as well. Petey Booker had followed the man down the darkened back streets of post-war Sydney and stuck a military bayonet into his spine. He'd left it there, a punctuation mark in the man's back. He'd then taken the man's money. Seven weeks after that, his mother had arranged from him to live with her American-by-marriage sister in Chicago to spare him a life of crime. It hadn't quite worked out that way.

"Now, kid, Petey, listen. Use this gun. It's clean. No way to trace it. Throw it on the floor in the hotel room when you finish. And walk away. But make sure, Petey, make sure. We gotta have this guy, this Dominic Peletiere. Faggot name, faggot guy, but he's hurting business working with the blacks off the South Side, and it has to stop. The man says so. You do the job. Do it clean. Then take a couple weeks off. In Florida maybe. Then come see me at the club in Cicero. We'll have some veal. Great veal in that club! Okay, kid? You got all this?" The man pressed the .38 caliber Smith and Wesson into Petey's hands. Petey nodded, saying nothing. The man walked away satisfied.

Peter Coy Booker, illegitimate and one of nine half-

brothers, hated to be called Petey. He had no idea who his real father was, and he didn't care. But he was twenty, and he was tired of "Petey." After tonight, he intended to change a few things. He walked down the bitter cold December streets of Chicago and climbed into the beat-up Ford that belonged to him because he'd been strong enough to take it from his "uncle." His aunt was okay. But how she'd settled on a man who came out of the big war with only one leg and one eye was beyond thinking about. As for his aunt, she was a tricky little piece and could suck the skin right off his dick. She liked it rough, and he bloody well gave it to her.

He drove the Ford toward the Gold Coast hotel strip. Nice part of town, all decorated for Christmas on this cold, windy, but clear Yule season night. In the back seat lay a sawed-off 12-gauge pump shotgun. The .38 felt cold against his taut stomach, tucked into his belt under his shirt.

He parked the car two blocks from his destination and pulled the shotgun from the back seat. It had only a pistol grip for a stock and was easily concealed under his overcoat. He was wearing a very sharp-looking dark blue suit. The doorman said, "Good evening." Booker nodded. He rarely spoke, because his Australian accent was worse than a fingerprint. He crossed the festively decorated hotel lobby and walked directly to the stairway. Nobody at the lobby desk paid any attention to the sharply dressed young man with the ready smile. Booker walked up 14 flights of stairs and stepped into the hallway. At the far end was Room 1445. He had been provided with a key. He stood for a brief moment outside the door, reaching up to unscrew the nearest hall light. The hallway darkened. He stepped to the door, inserted the key, and shotgun ready, slipped into the hotel suite and closed the door behind him.

The suite was dark, except for a small lamp on a table. Nobody was in the outer sitting room. The bedroom door was nearly closed, a shaft of light knifing its way across the hall, an arrow leading to his target. He moved across the room, poked open the bathroom door. A large man was sitting on the toilet masturbating, a copy of Penthouse in his hand. Peter Coy Booker set about to establish his name. He stepped into the bathroom and brought the shotgun down across the bridge of the man's nose. Pants around his ankles, the less-than-efficient bodyguard slumped to the bathroom floor, his head and his hard-on hitting the floor at the same time. Blood ran onto the white tiles. He would live, but every time he masturbated in the future, he would get a headache.

Silently, Booker moved to the bedroom, pushing the door open once again with the snout of the shotgun. On the bed, a woman's pale white legs were spread wide, tiny slender ankles tied to the bedposts, wrists tied together over her head. She was very thin, a platinum blonde servicing an enormously fat gangster who was groveling at her breast while he tried to force his penis, semi-hard, into her. Even though she was open to him, he was grunting with exertion. She saw Booker, and her eyes widened, but not in fear. A heroin set lay discarded on the floor next to the bed. This woman had what she wanted.

"Goddammit, bitch, lift your hips, willya, for chrissakes? I wanna fuck that sweet 17-year-old ass of yours." Now Booker understood why penetration posed such a problem.

"Get up, Dominic." Booker felt strangely angry, not that he cared at all about the tiny blonde bound submissively to the bed. He just felt anger.

"What?! Who the fuck are you? Get out of here. Joseph! Hey, Joseph! Get the fuck in here!"

"Joseph's not coming, Mr. Peletiere. He's really not coming." Booker thought of the hapless bodyguard, trousers at his ankles. He grinned. A very nasty grin. The fat man on the bed, still lying on the girl, looked suddenly very frightened. But tough. So he tried to negotiate.

"How much they paying you, kid? I'll double it. Triple it. You can corn-hole this little girl here. There's ten grand cash in my wallet. What do you say?"

"Get up, Dominic."

The fat man struggled up from the bed, stumbled back against a chair, tripped, and finally sat in it, naked and bloated and deserving his fate. The blonde's hips moved up and down, and she gave him a drugged smile. Booker aimed the shotgun at the fat man in the chair and kept it there as he pulled the wallet, stuffed with bills, from the man's suit pants. He pulled the thick wad of 100's from the wallet and put it back into the pants pocket.

"You're kind of cute, honey. Whyn't you come untie my legs." The blonde still did not realize her immediate peril. Heroin does that. The man looked more confident now. He'd bought the hit man, or so he thought.

The 12-gauge roared out in the small room, twice sending heavy lead shot into the man's chest, blowing him and the chair straight over backward. Blood spattered the wall and the naked teenage addict on the bed. She began to scream, and the third shotgun round turned her into a bloody smear on the bed.

Booker, moving fast, was out of the suite and down the stairs to the street before the elevator, full of desk help and bellhops, arrived at suite 1445. Two weeks later, he left the United States for Sydney. He didn't return to Chicago until 1980. By then, nobody called him "Petey" anymore.

4

The Desert
October 16, 1992

Con Duggan took aim, the custom-built .475 Linebaugh steady in his hands, Steven Dye looking downrange with considerable interest.

"One hundred yards? Pretty long way for a handgun, isn't it?"

"Nope."

The gun roared, the recoil very strong, even in the experienced grip of a master pistoleer. "Jesus Christ, how do you hang onto that sucker, Con? More to the point, what the hell is it?"

"It's a rebuilt Ruger Biseley single-action, and it's the only handgun like it in the world. Want to try it?"

Steven Dye was trying to locate the downrange pistol target, looking to see where, if at all, the target had been hit. It was a male silhouette, a bad guy holding a shotgun.

"You missed, Con."

"No, I didn't."

"Well, I can't find the hole."

"Check the nose. Should be there."

Steven Dye adjusted the glasses, bringing the figure into stark clarity. He focused on the stocking cap, lowered a bit, and saw the hole. The target's face had no nose. Just a gaping hole where it should have been.

"Do you shoot everything that well?" He gave Con a look of sure interest, one shooter to another.

"I suppose I do, yes." The gun bucked again, and Steven Dye decided at that moment the recoil was more than he would be able to handle.

"That's quite a gun."

"Yes. Do you want to shoot it?"

"I don't think so, Con. I have pretty limited experience with handguns, and that one looks like more than I could handle."

"Yeah. I guess it is." A third, fourth, and fifth shot boomed across the cold, flat shooting area a mile from Hangar 21A. Con Duggan emptied the gun, put the brass in his pocket, and reloaded.

"It's not a six-shooter?" Steven Dye knew nothing about pistols.

"No. Five. This cartridge needs the extra steel in the cylinder. I'll show you later."

"Okay."

"What do you want to know, Mr. Dye?"

"I don't think I'm sure what you mean, Con."

"Yes you are. So why don't you just spit it out?"

"Okay. Tell me how it was that you could sit at dinner in 1972 with a guy we're going to try to kill in six days."

Con Duggan ran the cleaning rod over and over again through the barrel of the .475, until the white cotton patches came out as clean as they went in. Steven Dye watched the process, smoking a cigarette, tossing it away, smoking another. He was fascinated by Con's single-minded concentration on the weapon. He seemed to be alone here on the dessert, and in some strange way Steven didn't quite understand. Steven felt he was looking at something he shouldn't be. Something uniquely personal to Con Duggan. Con cleaned the weapon, to Steven's eyes, much the same way a man would caress a woman.

"Booker was running guns one way and drugs the other." Con did not look up from his chore as he spoke.

"What?"

"In 1972, when we had dinner, Booker and I. It was just shortly before I . . . before I left Southeast Asia for good."

Steven Dye did not press. He just puffed on his next cigarette.

"At the time, Booker was working for a big time drug dealer from Thailand. Somebody told me, and I don't remember who, that Booker made two million dollars, cash, every month."

"Holy shit!"

"Yeah, well, if shit can be holy, his was." As he talked, Duggan wiped down the pistol with a lightly oiled cloth.

"He carried a Swedish 'K' automatic. He wore snake-skin cowboy boots, and he had a personal 12-man body-guard, and a Chinese girl about 20 who used to sit at his side practically naked, so he could get at her whenever he wanted to. She looked dead, but she wasn't. He seemed to favor women who had no fucking idea where or who they were."

"How did you come to meet him?"

"I was delivering a truckload of weapons. I needed his okay to get through his . . . neighborhood?" Steven Dye laughed, and so did Con Duggan.

"Yeah. His neighborhood. He was a gangster, really. Still is, I suppose."

"What was he like?"

"Tough. Very tough. But very smooth, too. He has a way about him, even when he makes a woman get down on all fours so he can rest his boots on her pretty back."

"You saw him do that?"

"Oh, yeah. And more. He is without human emotions. He eats. He fucks. He makes money. Primarily, he kills, and that is how he makes his money. He has no particular credo or political view. If he likes a job, or the money is right, he does it. Nothing very sophisticated. You pay him, he shoots. Sometimes, he shoots without pay. But he is a very charming man. I can and have outshot him in competitions all over the world. He is, surprisingly, a gracious competitor. Go figure.''

"What did he talk about at that dinner in the fucker-brush?''

Con gave Steven Dye a slow look, a measuring look.

"He talked about the United States in Vietnam. He thought we were stupid to be there, that it was not possible to use surrogate armies in South Vietnam to defeat North Vietnam. He said the South Vietnamese were corrupt Catholics, and that in the end, North Vietnamese tanks would drive up and smash Saigon like a corrupt paper doll backed by a corrupt American commitment. He was right.''

"You believed that?''

"No. Not then. But now, yes, I believe that. Vietnam shouldn't have happened. Not to the United States. But it did. And Booker enriched himself. But what the hell, who didn't?''

"You. You didn't.''

"Well, I might have—if I'd have understood what the fuck was going on. It was a war we could never have won. Not letting the South Vietnamese fight it. It was, in fact, doomed from the start. And I won't ever talk about Vietnam again.''

Steven Dye flipped his cigarette into the sand and lit another. "How about Booker.''

"Booker. Well, him we need to talk about—so we can try to kill him.''

By late evening of October 16th, 1992, the team so fragilely put together at great expense by the United States had loaded its combined weaponry and technicians onto the black-painted C-130 transport aircraft. The two men most responsible for the justification for all this expensive hardware boarded the plane to check it out after loading was completed. Satisfied that all they needed was aboard and accounted for, they went their separate ways for the night. They were to fly from the dessert at 0800 hours the next day. Each man knew that the success of their first team mission, on such short notice, and so little information, was likely to determine the future of the group. Con Duggan wished they had more time. Steven Dye was hot to go, an eager beaver with no real idea of what he would be called on to do.

Steven Dye had a secret. His real name should have been Bladen. Steven Bladen. If his erratic genius father had ever married his equally quixotic mother. Her last name had been Dye. Melody Dye, of the Berkeley hippy Dye's. Gypsies who spent most of their time in coffee houses or protest marches. Tuna versus dolphins. Drift nets. The forests. Nuclear power. Donald Anthony Bladen had been a disinterested observer to Melody Dye's escapades. His interest was pure and lustful. He was a musician with a Master's Degree, to add to a doctorate in physics. He preferred music, however, even though he occasionally took work designing super-secret munitions to keep his hand in.

Steven Dye's father had met his mother across a screaming line between the pro-nukes and the anti-nukes. She was taking time off that week from protesting the Vietnam War. Melody Dye had flame-red hair and a startling, whip-thin, but somehow lush-looking body. She had been in school off and on for over twenty years when she met Steven's father while swinging an anti-nuke poster at his studious-looking, bearded face. She had, in fact, hit him on the end of his nose before jumping on him piggyback style. Daniel Bladen took the opportunity to carry her away to the nearest bar to continue the argument. Screaming for help from her activist friends, Steven's mother had pummelled the broad back of his father with her tiny fists, the same hands she would use to pull him to her later that same night.

They loved each other, this rather odd couple, but there was a fairly serious problem in the way. Mr. Bladen was married to a Mrs. Bladen, who, incidentally, was the mother of his five little Bladens. She, the Mrs., was the rich offspring of two generations of rich Houston oilmen. In between babies, the Mrs. produced talk shows in Houston, taught at the university (psychology, sociology) and ran many of the charity organizations in that frantically rich city. She offered her trumpet-playing, sometime-defense-department-genius husband something no other woman could. Pedigree. And money. A hell of a lot of money. When Steven's father told his wife that he wanted to quit his life and move permanently to Berkeley with his semi-hippy consort, who, rather inconveniently, had become pregnant with yet another Bladen, the Mrs. was understandably angry. And when you are rich and angry, money, and the threatened prospect of not having any, sent the chastised Mr. Bladen to his now-rounded paramour, with time running out on the abortion possibilities.

She, Steven's mother, shocked everybody by saying she would keep her baby, thank you very much, and why don't you, Mr. Bladen, just fuck off. She would name the baby, and with a little help from a civil employee friend or two, give it her last name. And so she had. Steven Dye was born on October 21, 1968. While he did not have the Bladen name, or its marital money benefits, he did inherit something from his mostly absent father. A very keen mind, and a nature fit to turn that keenness loose on humanity. He liked weapons and wanted someday to design them, like his father.

Oh, yes. Young Steven not only knew who his father was, but saw him as often as possible after the premature death of his flamboyant mother, who died while trying to breathe with a mouthful of vomit in a drunken, three-day wipeout at Big Sur.

His father provided his son with the contacts and the money to go to MIT. Steven left that august institution with a Master's Degree and followed it with a doctorate, all by the time he was 20. He went immediately to work in super-sensitive labs, and then, before he had yet reached the ripe old age of 22, designed and produced the SIKIM-1000 for the Defense Intelligence Agency, ultimately resulting in his teaming with a craggy-faced veteran over twice his age for the purpose of assassination and mayhem.

That, bare bones, was his history. Technically a bastard child, ultimately acknowledged, if only in secret. Sent to the right schools, ushered into the deepest and most sophisticated espionage labs in the world, still carrying the last name of a woman who had given her bright mind and faith over to booze and drugs and excess.

There was, however, a great deal more to Steven Dye besides bare-boned history. He, like his father, was musically inclined, and could play a fair jazz guitar if asked. But most of what he was he got from his mother. He was, in spite of the brash red-headed expressions of flamboyant energy, if not downright bad attitude, a very sensitive, sometimes easily hurt personality. He was viewed as a ladies man by his male friends as well as his female acquaintances. He was not in truth. Women made him feel insecure, even awkward. He hid much of this partly because he hid most everything he was that resembled his mother. Behind her flaming star, too, there had been tragic vulnerability. To men, to society, to drugs and alcohol. Steven Dye felt he would someday wind up like his mother. A key element of his subterfuge was the constant talk of a mystical "father," Benjamin Dye, a creature of such mythically fraudulent credentials that his existence seemed completely plausible. So much had been made up about Benjamin Dye that Steven often got his own lies tangled. He now simply put him as "working for tribesmen in the upper Amazon." Most people took him at his word.

It was this mixed bag of psychological imprints that now was expected to perform at a high level of confidence in stressful situations. He seemed eager to everyone he encountered. Testing had shown him to have the needed profile. Inside, in secret, he was a mounting mass of self-doubt.

Con Duggan should have been back at Nellis Air Force Base, and Hangar 21A, preparing for the next day's flight to England. But Maggie, his Maggie, had flown all the way to Las Vegas to see him, and she expected to see him. She knew nothing about his newest venture with the government, and would not ask. He'd told her she could come and see him while he "tinkered around" in the desert.

They had met at the Vegas Hotel, and, understandably, since they were in love, even after eighteen years together, they went straight to her hotel suite and made love.

It had been, to Maggie, a happy surprise. Con had carried her along with him with more intensity than he had shown in a very long while. Like all long-time lovers, sex between then had become, well . . . if not exactly dull, at least predictable.

Con had grabbed her the minute they closed the hotel suite door behind them. She was wearing a lightweight dress, and he had pushed her down on the carpet and pulled her dress above her hips, practically tearing her French-cut panties from her full buttocks. Then he'd stood up after kissing her with such desperate longing that she'd simply lain sprawled where he left her on the rug. In seconds he was nude.

He'd joined her on the rug, first turning her over on her stomach, then pulling her up on her hands and knees, and he filled her almost immediately. She had been wet and ready, and it had been near violence as she looked back over her shoulder, her eyes glazed with lust, her hips churning backward at him, her ass raised high until she'd eventually put her face against the rough carpeting, saying over and over, "Do me, fuck me, do me, fuck me." Then she'd burst into climactic tears as he'd crashed into her, shouting her name.

"My, my, my," Maggie sighed as she regained her composure.

"Yeah, well, I guess I was horny."

Con's handprints were red and visible against the white skin of her hips, stark evidence of his ardor. Most of Maggie's body was tan to one shade or another, particularly her arms and face, but her buttocks were milk white. She was still lying on the gray rug, sweat glistening off her body in the light cast by the small table lamp next to the bed. A bed, she mused, that they hadn't even waited to reach. Con was kneading her flushed body like bread dough, his fingers bringing her a quirky combination of relaxation and sexual tension. "Still horny, I'd say," she said, a look of wonder on her face.

She reached back and began to stroke him. She rolled with him, not letting him go as she rode to yet another miraculous, exploding climax.

"I should come more often, Con. I mean to Las Vegas." They had finally climbed up to the bed and now lay on its crisp, white sheets, the bedspread tossed to the floor. She chuckled in the throaty way he loved, because it was one more natural way she did things. She chuckled. How many women, he wondered, "chuckle." Titter. Giggle. All that stuff, yes. But only Maggie chuckled.

"I love you, Maggie."

"I love you too, Con. Now what is this all about?" She struggled up from his arms and sat cross-legged at his side, her blue eyes studying his face, her black hair wild and mussed, the ends still clinging to her shoulders from the sweat generated by their frantic lovemaking.

"I don't know what you mean, Maggie. What is *what* all about?"

"Sex. This *kind* of sex. We used to have it like this once a day. But that was 15 years ago. What is *this* all about is what I mean." She fixed his eyes with hers and did not break eye contact. She wanted to know. And he wanted to tell her. So he tried.

"Well, the sex was great, but I'm not exactly sure why, I mean, why it was *that* great."

"Con . . ."

"Okay. I'm leaving. In the morning. For about a week. No big deal." He gave her a weak smile.

"I believe you're leaving, Con, but I don't believe for a minute that you think it's no big deal. You're back in it, aren't you, Con? You're going to shoot. Am I right?"

Well, there it was, he thought. She wants to know, and you aren't supposed to tell anyone. Not even Maggie. Perhaps not. But Maggie needed to know, and she would read a lie, because she loved him.

"I'm going to England to stop an assassination attempt against the Prime Minister and the President of France."

"What?"

"Yeah, that essentially is it. I've joined a new team headed by Michael Barns. You knew that."

"Yes, I knew that. I didn't know, however, what this 'new team' was scheduled to do. How can this be, Con? The United States has no authority in England."

"That's true. We don't. We'll work with them, I guess. It's unlikely our team will provide any more than . . . uh, than guidance."

"Guidance?" Maggie's voice reeked with sarcasm.

"Yeah, you know, intelligence and stuff. Hell, Maggie, you know about this business. Your dad's a United States Senator for Christ sakes! You've been around this all your life."

"Yes. I have. And I left it to be with you out in the bushes. And now you're leaving me to play this stupid, macho kid's game. Didn't you have enough in Vietnam? Don't you remember all that, Con? Goddamn you!"

"Honey, I . . . honey, ah, Mags, listen to me—"

"No! You listen to me! You can't throw me on the floor and fuck me to make me pliant. Was that it? Is that why your dick was so hard and good, Duggan? Let's just throw Maggie a fuck and she'll shut her mouth and go away happy? Is that what this lovely fucking is all about?"

"No, Maggie, that's not what it's about. It was that good, that strong, because I'm scared to death of what I'm doing." He gazed at her, his eyes sad and resigned, the look of a man telling the truth. And a hard truth at that.

"You—afraid?" To Maggie, that was an impossible thought.

"Why not, Maggie? I have no idea what will happen. I have no idea if I can cut it anymore. And for my own sanity, I have to find out. I suppose, truth told, I threw you on the floor to prove I'm still a man. And all it proved was that I can get it up when I look at you. Cheap trick, I know. I figured I wouldn't be scared. But I am, Maggie. I really am." His gaze remained steady on her face, searching her eyes for, for . . . what?

Maggie had been with Con Duggan for 18 years. They had built a home for themselves, both literally and figuratively. They had done all this in the growing sense of oneness they shared. The recovering Con Duggan, out of the hospital, even though still badly scarred, if not visibly, had wanted no more than to be with her. To forget. To walk away. He had done enough.

And she had accepted that. Dumped a promising career as a lawyer. Broken with her hawklike father. Just the wilds of Alaska, her home, and the strong, quiet man she loved at her side. Now, she could feel it slipping away, in his haunted eyes. Her lover. Her man. Her everything. And yet, this was the first time in their life together he had been so naked before her. Psychologically naked and vulnerable. She knew at that moment that with one word she could take him back to Alaska and away from whatever he was unsure about. Back to cookies and tits, as Con so graphically put it. Well, yes, she could obviously, this one time, use his love for her and make him do what *she* needed him to do. Of course, one day he could hate her for it. She had to let him go his way.

"Con, I don't believe you are afraid. You are *afraid* to fail. That's not the same, because I know you. And you will *not* fail, whatever the outcome. Your ghosts are all buried. And if not, you'll deal with them. I know you will." She bit her lip, fighting back tears, resisting the urge to beg and plead and go all-female on him. His gaze remained steady. Without words, he pulled her down to his chest, and she wept the tears of the self-sacrificing.

Enroute To England
October 17, 1992

The big jet transport flew toward Europe at an easy 560 knots at 30,000 feet with no rush to get there. It was packed to the wingtips with electronic gear and computers. It was a flying intelligence center capable of sending, receiving, and analyzing messages from and about anyplace in the world. It was scheduled to land at a military base near London where Con and Steven Dye were to meet an elite British counterterrorist unit to compare notes and strategies, which Con Duggan thought was pretty funny, since at the moment, he had damn little of each to compare.

Con sat in one of the comfortable, couch-like seats in the aircraft's center section, studying a 90-page intelligence update on Peter Coy Booker. Not a thing in it was of any value.

The jet's engines droned on, the white-shirted technicians in the forward compartment bent to their mysterious, electronic tasks. Con Duggan lit a cigarette, leaned back in his chair, and tried to remember what he knew about Booker.

Southeast Asia
1972

"You bloody Yanks haven't got chance one out here, don't you know that?" Con stared at the bare-chested Aussie through the slitted eyes of a man trying not to lose his Yankee cool. But this Booker guy was surely trying what little patience he had left.

"Now you take those trucks full of M-16s over there. The U.S. paid for the bloody things! You give them to regional forces to keep the fucking commies at bay. Right? Am I right? Don't bother to answer, Mr. Duggan. You give them to village chiefs, they give them to me for, how should I say . . . security reasons, and—"

"By that," interrupted Con, *"you mean you promise not to kill them and destroy their village."*

"Well, it rarely comes to that, now does it? Let's just say we make a deal. Then I and my merry band take these fine United States examples of craftsmanship halfway across bloody Asia. The Iron Triangle people are grateful. We get the poppy trade, and they get the weapons to wage little gang wars on one another. Bloody tidy, don't you think?"

"And you, Booker. How much do you make on this deal?"

"Ah . . . money. Well, I make quite a kit, actually. But that's free enterprise. The American Way, brought to Southeast Asia by a Chicago-raised Aussie. Bloody wonderful world, isn't it? And let's not forget what I give back, eh, Con Duggan, USMC. I gave your people the last ten of your targets, remember? And tomorrow, you will thrash bravely forward into the dank underbrush of Cambodia to slay the dragon queen herself. Thanks to my information. So while I know you personally disapprove,

*you, after all, take your . . . your pound of flesh, shall we
call it?''*

*Enraged, Con lunged toward Booker, but Booker was
very fast, and his two silent but efficient bodyguards were
even faster. Con was clubbed to the ground and found
himself pinned by his arms and legs. He struggled to get
free, but it was useless. Booker, standing at the outer
reach of the firelight, pulled the slim, pliant Chinese
woman to him and waved a hand in dismissal, a lord
dispatching, or dispensing, leniency.*

*''Let him up, mates. I may need him someday.'' He
tugged the drugged girl after him into the darkness, a
man of overpowering evil able to walk his way throughout the world because he understood its ways better than
the good guys.*

*Con Duggan spent the night staring into the campfire.
In the morning, the weapons trucks pulled out, and Con
Duggan set out after his 100th kill and a period of time
in his life more painful than death.*

Con snapped out of his reverie with a start as Steven
Dye removed the cigarette that had burned down to a nub
from between Con's fingers.

''You're about to blister your trigger finger, Con.
Can't have that now, can we?''

''Sorry. I was trying to figure out why in God's name
I allowed myself to be conned back into this business.''

'' 'Conned' is the word all right.'' Steven Dye sat
down, an inquisitive smile on his face. ''Why did you?''
Steven Dye expected no real answer to his question. He
was not disappointed.

''Stupid. Drunk. Senile. Who knows?''

''Okay. I'll let it go.''

''Good idea, Mr. Dye.''

''Speaking of good ideas, do you have any?''

''Not at the moment, no.'' Con Duggan was not re-
freshed by his memories of Peter Coy Booker.

''Well, I have one.''

''Fine, Steven, I'm all ears.''

"Yes. They *are* large, but I digress. Why the fuck don't the British just grab this guy? Arrest him."

"On what charge, Mr. Dye?"

"Charge? Who the fuck cares! Pick one! Violation of good taste for being born in a colony. Pimping, shoplifting, what difference does it make, Con? Hell, he's a threat to their national security. Lock him up for a week and then kick him loose."

"It wouldn't be legal, and it wouldn't work, and I suspect most of all, the Brits would like to find out who hired him to do this."

"So you're telling me they will allow the Prime Minister and the President of frogs to just get killed in the interest of finding out who fronted the money?"

"I believe the British expect *us* to find out. One other thing. I have some very nasty memories of this guy, my young associate. And I say this. He's not doing it alone, and we don't yet know *how* he's going to do it. Arrest him, and it just might happen anyway. No, the key to this little problem—"

"Little problem! Jesus, Con!" Steven Dye nearly jumped out of his chair with youthful indignation.

"As I was saying, this little exercise has a simple key. Stop Mr. Booker by killing him and his team. That is as subtle as I can get at the moment. Now go away, Steven. I need sleep. We will see what Brit intelligence has and work from there."

Con Duggan went back to his study of the useless printout on Peter Coy Booker. Steven Dye shut up, but he stayed in his chair. Finally, he fell asleep in it, his red hair tousled against his shoulder, his legs tucked up like a child. Con thought he looked positively angelic. Without thinking, he tossed a Navajo blanket over his sleeping teammate. A father-to-son gesture, if he'd considered it.

Con Duggan put the report on Booker aside and closed his eyes even though he didn't expect to actually sleep. The drone of the plane's powerful engines coursed through his brain, and his body resonated with the plane's vibrations. It wasn't an unpleasant sensation.

Duggan let his mind drift toward their arrival. It would be late on Friday evening. Their big briefing at British Intelligence was scheduled for Monday morning. But there would be more than enough to occupy them over the weekend. For one thing, there was the arrival of the C-130 on Saturday. And then perhaps a visit to a few of London's ubiquious pubs. . . . Yes, that was something to look forward to. Especially since he knew what else was coming.

London
October 20, 1992

The intelligence agencies of the United Kingdom were housed in a tall, glass-encased building in Central London, a curious appendage thrust up like a middle finger among the more traditional tourist expectations surrounding it. The building contained most, if not all, arterial connections between Britain and its diminishing foreign interests. Britain had a "special relationship" with the United States, but it was a relationship in name, memory, and nostalgia only. Still, the American people and the British people were more often than not of a like mind in most things.

At the lower or middle official echelons, however, the British still felt, without much justification, superior to their former colonies, and they considered the United States a former colony. Stiff upper lips abounded. Most particularly, they held sway in the traditional MI-5 and MI-6 intelligence sections of the British governmental structure.

Guided by a dour-faced functionary, Con Duggan and Steven Dye were ushered into a world of long hallways, narrow doors without markings, and elevators to nowhere. The modern glass exterior of the building hid a near-Victorian interior of cramped spaces and cramped, pinched-in functionaries seemingly extracted intact from the past.

The women, and there appeared to be a staggering

number of them, wore their hair pulled back and little, if any, makeup. They projected a generally suppressed air, servants to equally repressed, blank-faced men. Only after a dizzying journey through clouds of clerks and floor after floor of 1950's decor, were the two men ushered into the more modern yet equally gray and sanitary world of computerized intelligence. The four upper floors of the building held chicly dressed men and mini-skirted women intent on servicing a large number of squat, imposing machines. It was as if the bottom of the building had been squeezed very hard, like a tube of toothpaste, and at the top, the clear gray form of the future face of Britain had spurted out, leaving the lower floors flat in comparison. Smiles, it seemed, were mandatory at the top of the intelligence tube.

"Ah, good to meet you chaps! Farquarson, here! Reggie most of the time. How about it? Reggie, I mean. And you, you must be Steven Dye!" The man looked positively, radiantly informed. Unfortunately, he was enthusiastically pumping Con Duggan's hand. "Ah, yes, and you would be Con Duggan. Smashing! Absolutely smashing to meet you!" He nearly separated Steven Dye's arm from his shoulder in greeting.

Steven Dye couldn't resist. He slipped into a fairly good impersonation of an Englishman and said, "Oh, I say, chap, you've got us bloody well mixed up, sorry to say. The *old* gent is Con Duggan. *I* am Steven Dye."

"Oh! Oh, well, I say, chaps, our intelligence isn't near as good as it's cracked up to be, is it? I say, it seems I've been misinformed, doesn't it?"

Con gave Steven a very strange look. Steven, for his part, could only wonder what they could possibly expect to accomplish if Farquarson was to be their contact.

"Bloody embarrassing, chaps. But let's get along, shall we? Madeline, pump up what we have on this situation, will you? Mister Dye," here Farquarson nodded toward Steven, "and Mr. Duggan," another nod, this time toward Con, "will need our most informed help in their dangerous visit to our tight little island." Madeline, a comely blonde with short heels to match her skirted, long pale legs, hit a switch, and the gray eminence of computer banks began to whirl and spit out whistles and bells of information. All of it useless to Con Duggan.

"Well now, chaps, is that a help? Well, of course it is!" Farquarson said when the screens finally went blank.

"Mr. Farquarson, I think—"

"Reggie. Please, call me Reggie."

"Right. Reggie. Since we are now pals and comrads, what the hell was I to gain from that report that I don't already know?"

"Pardon?" Reggie gave Con Duggan a quizzical look. An old-maiden-aunty look, the one you get when you have criticized her cookie recipe by not eating any cookies.

"Do you have any information that will actually assist us in stopping this man?"

"Well, of course we do! Whatever do you think we do here? Madeline, tell these ... these *people* what we have."

Madeline, she of the long legs, short skirt, and bunned hair, whipped out a yellow lined pad and began to read it. Steven Dye tried to listen without seeming to stare at her garters, blue-black with red bows.

"We believe there are at least seven and perhaps thirteen members of Mr. Booker's team. We have identified, confirmed, six of the team as being in the UK, either in London, Wales, or Edinburough. We have assigned thirty ... no ... thirty-one agents to monitor their every move. I myself took one of these gentlemen to bed only three days past. Unfortunately, I gained neither sexual satisfaction nor precise information."

"Did he enjoy himself?" Steven Dye had turned into a loose cannon with a smirk. Madeline shifted her hips on the desk edge, revealing two inches of creamy thigh untouched by the sun.

"Yes, I believe he did. May I go on?" She gave Steven Dye a look of complete and utter contempt sprinkled with a bit of lust. Con Duggan, over fifty, could only wish he were twenty-two again.

"Please, Madeline, do go on." Reggie Farquarson looked like a mouse freed from a cheesy trap. Madeline resumed her report and managed for the moment to look professional in spite of her legs.

"We know the Prime Minister and the French President will be safe. They will be in the Chunnel, free from assault, for 62 of the 71 minutes they will spend together. When they return to their respective homes, they will do so by helicopter with massive air protection. They will be vulnerable only before they enter the tunnel on the French side and when they exit the tunnel on the English side. There will be a massive security presence on each side of the channel."

"Then why did you ask for our help?" Con Duggan had only one question he needed answered, and that was it.

Madeline shifted uneasily, tugging at her skirt, her eyes searching for Reggie's.

"Well, Mad, why not tell them? I believe Mr. Duggan suspects, anyway. Don't you, Mr. Duggan?" Not a question at all. Madeline, free from responsibility for the truth, told the truth.

"We have decided, in effect, to use this . . . this *occasion*, to destroy Mr. Booker and his team. We understand you know Mr. Booker personally. We need you to assist us in . . . in . . ."

"Killing him?"

"Quite right. Killing him."

"Killing them all, you mean."

"That would be nice, yes." Her lower lip quivered in anticipation.

To Steven Dye, Maddy didn't look nearly as desirable as she had only a moment before. She had terrific, gartered legs, and no soul whatsoever.

"Do we have TAP photos?"

Maddy looked at Con Duggan, not sure what he meant.

"Target Acquisition Points."

"Oh! Yes, two thousand or more. But we have *not* done TAP photos for you or . . . or . . ."

"Dye. Steven Dye."

"Yes. Dye. Steven Dye. We felt if you're going to . . . to . . ."

"Kill them?"

"Quite. Yes, quite. You should decide how you want . . . how you want to . . ."

"Kill them?"

"Yes, quite so. Kill them. Indeed."

"Madeline is a good sort, actually, Mr. Duggan. She's just very young. Sex, of course. She has it, now doesn't she? But killing, well, she *is* young. Much like your Mr. Dye, if I'm any judge."

"Farky?" Con had chosen a name he liked. And it fit.

"Yes?"

"You're a terrific judge of youthful character. We, you and I, shall have to lead the lambs to the butcher."

"Oh, yes, quite! I quite agree! More Scotch?"

"Ah, yes, definitely more Scotch." Con Duggan, clasped in the soft leather of a London club chair, accepted his fifth Laphroaig Scotch, $4.00 a shot in the States. A life he could get used to.

"Hey, Farser."

"Yes, Duggy?"

"I'm shitfaced, but I'm about to make a pledge."

"I say! A pledge is it? Well then, Duggy, drink up, and pledge away!"

"Fine. I can only promise you blood, sweat, and tears. Not to mention how much is owed by so few to so many!"

"Oh, I say, smashing! So few to so many! A smashing twist, that! Winnie, rest his soul, would have loved it."

"Here's to Winnie. And his soul." Con raised his glass.

"Winnie's soul!" The glasses clinked. The men passed out.

• • •

"So, Mr. Dye, have you done this sort of thing for quite a long time?" Madeline's tongue flicked out, tasting a bead of sweat from her nose.

"What sort of thing, Maddy?"

"Spy things. You know." Steven Dye strained forward, his arms rippled with youthful muscles he didn't know he had.

"Oh, spy things ... Well, not long, but I think you should ... yes, I think you should ..."

"What, Steven? What should I do?" Her legs spread wide, pulling him to her. She dug her patent leather heels into his buttocks.

"Get on top this time." Steven was gasping for breath, and leverage.

"Fine ... yes ... but not *this* time. Next time, maybe." At that moment, Madeline's body swallowed Steven Dye whole.

Con Duggan woke up with a very big, Scotch-induced headache. He was not sure where he was, but somewhere in the background, Etta James was singing "Misty" with considerable blues power. He liked Etta James. For the briefest second, he wondered just exactly how the British intelligence service had discovered that. A very proper, butler-type Englishman handed him a cup of American coffee and informed him he had a meeting in one hour with "Farky." His clothes were laid out neatly over a mahogany service stand. As he dressed, Etta sang on.

"Get up, lazy bones."

Steven Dye opened first one eye, then reluctantly the other. Madeline, dressed in a leather mini-dress, smiled down at him and offered him coffee. He asked for a drink.

"Now, you Yanks! Shame! Coffee, darling. Farquarson and your Mr. Duggan are waiting for us. Hurry along now!" Her trim, exotic body swung its compact way out of view. She had changed her garter belt. Today it was purple, with white stockings. He was definitely not in Kansas anymore. Of course, he never had been.

"The Garden Coast, chaps. Enjoy!" Reggie Farquarson, in his home-movie mode, spoke with a strangely professional, tour-guide voice as Con Duggan and Steven Dye were introduced to what Peter Coy Booker hoped would be a happy hunting ground.

"Mile upon mile of sandy beaches, a wonderful playground for children, just made for building sand castles. Fun-fairs geared for all ages. A ride on the Romney, Hythe, and Dymchurch Railway."

"Dimcurch!" said Steven. Farky gave Steven Dye a very severe, very British look.

"Quite so! Now, if you'll allow me to proceed."

"By all means, Reggie," said Con Duggan. "We are, both of us, all eyes."

The movie rolled on. Sissinghurst Gardens, White Castle Gardens, Scotney Castle Gardens. Churches . . . St. Peters, St. Eanswythe, All Souls, Holy Trinity, St. Paul's, Little Switzerland, Lympne Zoo. Ferry Terminal, Eastcliff Sands.

"Reggie, what do all these places have in common, if anything?"

"An astute question, Con. They are, each of them, potential assassination areas. Conversely, they are Target Acquisition Points for you. Somewhere in all these areas, and somehow, you will have to locate the villains and kill them, one at a time, in the 61 minutes you have while the Prime Minister and the French President are traveling through the Chunnel. Sixty one minutes. That is it. You must find somewhere between seven and thirteen assassins led by Peter Coy Booker, and slay them, for God and the UK. Now may I go on?"

The movie and the narration continued. "This is Leas Cliff hall in Folkstone. This week, the Euro-militaire, a military figurine exhibition, will be held. Two thousand hobbyists from all over the world will be here, displaying, buying, selling, trading. Your target will be there.

Quite a cover, don't you think? He has the largest collection of military models in the world, including over 200 soldiers, I'm told, that Mr. Booker made himself. Some of the exhibitors, we believe, are part of his team. Also, his yacht *Stingray* will drop anchor in Folkstone Harbor tomorrow morning. It is 106 feet long, carries a crew of twenty-seven, and space for God-knows-what. We hope you will find time to *sink* her in some way. Now, are there any questions?''

''Yeah ... How do I get out of this chickenshit outfit?'' Steven Dye gave Con Duggan a look to remember.

Folkstone, England
October 21, 1992

The 106-foot-long motor yacht *Stingray*, Booker at the helm, slipped into Folkstone Harbor, as promised by Reggie Farquarson, at 10:00 A.M. the next day. The day was bright and cloudless, but there was no warmth to the sun that splashed across the tiered hillsides of Folkstone, Kent, the Garden Coast of England.

Small stubborn puffs of color clung to the East Cliff sands, Sea Point, and below Sandgate Castle. The *Stingray* had cruised up and down the Folkstone coastline as Booker took his own TAPs. Photos from the seaside he would later determine to be of no help to him at all. But he wasn't worried. Booker had over thirty men with him and more than that on shore eager to open doors, if not roadways, for the right sum.

He turned the sleek craft back over to its Filipino captain and went below to prepare his exhibit for the Euro-militaire at Leas Cliff Hall, only twenty minutes' walk from his moorage. It took no effort whatever to shift to his usual, glad-handing style as he went ashore. He was, after all, one of the world's premier collector/builders of military models.

Dorsey followed his boss ashore, wearing only a combat knife in his boot. For some reason, Booker had ordered his six-man party not to carry weapons. Odd. And Dorsey disobeyed, as Booker knew he would.

Fifteen minutes later, Booker and his party were met by over thirty English policemen in plain clothes. His passport and those of his nattily dressed group were scrutinized with particular care. Jade, the exotic Cambodian woman Booker was presently using had shot herself full of heroin only moments before she disembarked from the *Stingray*. She could barely stand up, and she clung to Booker, her hard nipples pressing against the thin silk of her dress, a black and silver creation slit to the thigh. He had expected police scrutiny. If it had not happened, he would have dropped the contract immediately.

"Well, Mr. Booker, we are happy to see you. Please forgive the rather extensive use of police, but the Prime Minister herself will be here in five days' time. Of course, you knew that, didn't you?"

"And why, Inspector, would I know that? I'm here for the exhibition at Leas Cliff Hall. I was here in '90 as well. And I am sure you know that."

"Yes. Well, we are happy to see you your lovely boat once again. If we can be of service to *any* of your group, please let us know." The inspector gave the drugged-out Jade a meaningful look. She only giggled.

"By the way, Mr. Booker, this knife was found on the marine walk, just below our present position. You wouldn't recognize it, would you? I mean, is it yours?" The eight-inch, ivory-handled knife was clearly Dorsey's.

"Yes, it is a knife I recognize. I suspect Mr. Dorsey here dropped it. He will need it to open the twenty or so packing cartons we have shipped to Leas Cliff Hall. Dorsey! Come on, man, let's not be so careless in the future! Please, Inspector, accept our apologies. Another Aussie misbehaves in the mother country. Well, you except that from us, don't you, Inspector?" Booker gave the inspector a smile from somewhere beyond the grave.

"We are at your service, Mr. Booker." The inspector handed the wicked-looking knife to Booker, and he and his men walked away toward Folkstone Police Station, only two-hundred-yards distant.

Booker gave Dorsey a blistering stare and without comment handed him his forbidden knife. The small group entered Leas Cliff Hall in less than ten minutes. Discovered, of course. But he'd expected that. Booker was satisfied. He looked forward to the fine exhibition at Leas Cliff Hall, his own collection the centerpiece. Perhaps he might finally make a trade with the obnoxious seaman with the exquisite World War II Tiger tank models. In some things, Peter Coy Booker was an honorable man.

6

Twenty minutes after Booker's party encountered the plain-clothes police officer, Con Duggan and Steven Dye drove down Shorncliff Road and turned right onto Castle Hill Avenue, headed toward the Langhorne Gardens Hotel. A good American League outfielder or a strong-armed NFL quarterback could have hit Booker at Leas Cliff Hall with a well-directed ball of either sport from Langhorne Gardens. Steven Dye had driven the hot little BMW, but not very well. He kept missing the gears, trying to go fast. Finally, Con had made him stop on M-20, the equivalent of I-5 in the States, and taken over the driving chores in the hope they would both arrive safely. Which they did. From that moment on, they would not be safe again.

The Langhorne Gardens Hotel was situated only 75 yards from the exhibition to be held at Leas Cliff Hall and looked down on it, particularly from the third floor suite Con and Steven occupied. A rifle shot beyond Leas Cliff, the massive bulk of Booker's 106-foot *Stingray* dwarfed

69

all other boats in the harbor. From their suite, Con and Steven could look into her heart, if not her soul.

The *Stingray* had a very impressive exterior. Painted a startling white, she looked bigger than she was, and she was big in reality as well. She was mostly wood, and her exposed wooden surfaces were polished to a high gloss and kept that way by a ten-man crew that had been selected by Booker on the basis of how good they were at the job and nothing else. They crewed the elegant yacht but were not involved in any of Booker's outside activities. The *Stingray* had sailed the equivalent of ten trips around the world in the twenty years she had sailed under Booker's Australian flag that was accompanied by a black flag with a large white "B" superimposed on a map of Australia. The *Stingray* was well known in many ports of the world, some less available to the general boating public than others.

The *Stingray* had carried contraband of one kind or another to every continent. In its hold and on its deck, six Zodiac outboard-powered boats had hauled dope, guns, and women from ship to shore and back again. The sleek yacht had prowled all the world's oceans and many of its rivers. In addition to its ten-man crew, it usually hauled anywhere from seven to thirty armed mercenaries to wherever there was money to be made. A complement of Booker's favorite women provided the ship's sexual menu, paid according to their individual needs.

Some of these young women needed dope. Cocaine or heroin or whatever the popular drug of the year might be. Some needed shelter, money, love, or excitement. The *Stingray* in one way or another satisfied all their needs. And Booker's as well, whose sexual needs required a large number of disparate women at his beck and call. The women were like assorted candies in a gift box. Some were hard, some were soft, some were fattening. All were tasty.

The *Stingray* had awesome defensive armaments in keeping with her illicit travels throughout a dangerous world of criminal and political activities. Fifty caliber machine-guns were mounted under innocent-looking lifesaving equipment storage bins, able to be brought to bear from no less than six combat stations ingeniously built into the *Stingray* both fore and aft.

She carried sea mines, anti-tank weapons, Russian-made grenade launchers, and every variety of firearm from assault rifle to crossbow. On this particular trip, the *Stingray* carried a boat crew of ten, six women, and a twenty-man hit team versed in handling every weapon on the yacht. An international consortium of banking interests had prepaid Peter Coy Booker twenty-five million dollars to attack the British Prime Minister and the French President. That was a mistake ... Peter Coy Booker, prepaid, didn't care whether he was successful or not. Prepaid, this exercise for him was a game, a kind of stretching of his intellectual muscle against the impossible hit. But if it proved impossible, he knew he could simply glide out of Folkstone Harbor untouched and twenty-five million richer. As for the men who had been coerced into prepaying this jaunt to the Garden Coast of England, they ... well, they were very much easier to kill. And comfortingly enough, they knew that. If he could make it work, fine. If not, sail on, sail on, oh ship of state.

From the three-cornered window of the Langhorne Gardens Hotel, Con Duggan swept the decks of the *Stingray* with a beat-up old pair of WWII German binoculars given to him by his father over forty years ago. They had once belonged to a famous *Waffen SS* tank commander. His father never told Con how he got them, but he'd had a grim, tight little smile on his face when he handed them to his then twelve-year-old son. Six months later, his father had placed the barrel of a revolver in his mouth and pulled the trigger, taking his life to end the pain of a cancer eating away at his stomach and intestines that would have killed him in weeks anyway.

Con and his mother had stood at the gravesite with the

large, Catholic Duggan family, their faces stern with disapproval of the father's action. Con's mother, a tough,
ruddy-cheeked Scot, had held her son's hand very tightly.
She had not cried, and neither had Con. A typical,
drunken Irish wake followed, because funerals were for
getting on with life, not to celebrate its end. Finally, when
his mother got back to their small house, she had sat the
young Con Duggan down and told him about how really
wonderful his father had been. Then, and only then, did
the surviving Duggans cry.

"What's to see, Con?"

"Well, Mr. Dye, Peter Booker has a hell of a gorgeous
boat, populated by spiffy crewmen in whites, women in
not much, and a lot of places to hide damn near anything."

"Can I look?"

"Sure." Con Duggan handed the heavy binoculars to
his young associate and dropped himself solidly into his
chair and lit a cigarette. He had no idea what they should
do next.

"Well, well, look what we have here." Con glanced at
Steven Dye, noticed the glasses were pointed sharply
down, and stood up, placing himself behind Steven, who
was trying to line up the glasses and their target.

"What? What do we have?"

"Right across the street at the Exhibition Hall entrance. Mr. Booker and friends."

"Booker has no friends." Con Duggan was out the
door and headed toward Leas Cliff Hall before Steven
Dye realized he was gone.

The Euro-militaire Exhibition at Leas Cliff Hall would
surely have delighted any little boy and the little boy in
every man who viewed it. Even Con Duggan, whose
view of Peter Coy Booker had been obscured by a pha-
lanx of hangers-on as he entered the hall, was impressed
as he entered at a near sprint to catch up to his old
nemesis.

The hall fairly glittered with bright lights cast to highlight models of everything military. Tiny regiments of hand-carved, hand-painted soldiers marched valiantly forward across a green felt diorama of Napoleonic warfare. WWI tanks less than six inches long thrust forward against gray-helmeted troops of Kaiser Wilhelm. A glass case held two dozen models of WWI ambulances of detailed perfection, right down to the bloody floor only inches beneath the wounded men depicted so poignantly they could make you wince with pain or cry out in pity.

Scale models of aircraft hung from elevated platforms: fighters, bombers, even zeppelins. If you could imagine it, someone had probably crafted it.

U.S. Marines flung themselves at the coconut sea wall of Tarawa atoll in a six-feet-square diorama of detail so exquisite you could see wounded men falling back away from the wall, chopped down by withering fire from the barren acres of the Marines' terrible crucible of fire in WWII.

The exhibition was a tribute to the fighting men and women and machines of two thousand years of human conflict, all in exquisite miniature. But Con Duggan saw very little of it. He saw Booker, and without knowing what he intended to do, he crossed the exhibition hall floor until he was face to face with the man he had come to England to kill. Booker looked up at him, the briefest flicker of surprise in his eyes quickly extinguished. Booker gave Con a quiet look, an appraisal, and then extended his hand.

"Ah, Duggan, good to see you. Came to see the exhibit, did you? I didn't know you were interested in this sort of thing. But then, you have *wide* interests, don't you? Mia, let me introduce you to an old . . . an old what, would you say, Con?" Mia, an Oriental with surgically rounded eyes, gave Con a cool, uninterested look.

"Competitor. How about competitor?"

"Ah, yes. Well, competitor, this is Mia. I call her 'Missing in Action,' for short. Tell me, Duggan, what are you doing for dinner?"

"No plans."

"Good. Be down at the Harbor Station at six. I'll send a Zodiac to pick you up."

"Oh, is your toy boat here?"

"Really, Duggan. You're a card, aren't you? He's a card, Mia, isn't he? Didn't know the *Stingray* was here, eh? Well then, now you know. Six o'clock, then?"

"Six o'clock is fine." Con spun on his heel and walked away, the hot feel of the artificially bright lights of the hall burning down on him. Dinner on the *Stingray*. Sometimes things just worked out if you pushed hard enough.

The fast little Zodiac was right on time at Harbor Station Pier. A crisply dressed crewman pulled the boat to within jump-in distance. The weather was briskly cold, a hard black sky scattered with stars and fast-moving clouds. The wind came from all directions at once, and the harbor water had a nasty chop to it.

"I hate this already," Steven said.

"Wait a while. You'll hate it more."

"Two of you, sir? I wasn't told there would be two of you." The crewman had a sing-song Caribbean accent, an odd sound in the cold and dark of an English harbor.

"Two of me? No, there is only one of me, and one of him. Two each, separately, or whatever." Con Duggan kept his voice light, masking his worry.

"I'll have to check with the *Stingray* sir."

"Oh, yes, please do that. Tell Mr. Booker to set an extra plate. Surely he has an extra plate on board somewhere."

The crewman spoke into a hand-held radio in what appeared to be French. The reply took only a moment to materialize.

"Two of you, eh?" Booker's voice came loud and clear over the speaker on the Zodiac. "Well, why not? Any mate of Con Duggan's is a mate o'mine. Bring them, Baptiste." The speaker scratched once and then went silent.

"Well, Steven, you heard the man. Any mate of mine is a mate of his. All aboard for the lap of luxury."

The boat pulled away from the pier very rapidly, bucking across the waves toward the *Stingray*, moored only two hundred yards away, its lighted portholes and deck lights beckoning them on.

"Fucking bumpy lap, if you ask me," Steven said. "I'd die of illness if the damn boat was another hundred yards away." In spite of his tension, Con Duggan could only laugh into the wind at his irrepressible partner. Not much seemed to bother this kid.

Aboard The Stingray
Folkstone Harbor
October 21, 1992

Con attempted to survey the boat as they were led along its polished decks to a brass-railed, red-carpeted stairway and down into the middle deck area that functioned as Booker's one-hundred-six-foot-long floating home. He didn't expect to see anything that would help him in his mission, and he would have been very surprised if he had. It was what it seemed to be, a luxury yacht capable of powering her way to any port in the world.

But oh, what luxury. The walls of the companion ways were hung with original paintings on both sides, spaced so the viewer could pay attention to one without being distracted by the next. Paintings to savor. Chagal. Matisse. Degas. Piccasso. Steven Dye thought of himself as an art lover. But he had never seen these pictures on public display. He had no way of knowing that public display to Booker meant that *he* got to own and display them. For power points. Steven Dye was properly impressed.

The interior walls were a rich, if a bit gaudy, combination of shiny wood, powder-blue and gold walls, and everywhere a wine-red carpet that must have cost a thousand dollars a square foot.

Everywhere Booker's standard, his cry for recognition,

the white "B" over the Australian flag on a black field was embossed, painted, embroidered, or done in gold and precious stones. A massive ego was present here, the ego of a poor Australian kid who raped and murdered his way out of an Aussie ghetto by way of Chicago, in the process turning himself into one of the richest men in the world. What it said to Con Duggan, this vulgar display of a criminal's rise to power, was simple. Peter Coy Booker was, to most people, a man of sophisticated social skills made fraudulent by his need to advertise what he had, to hide what he was. There were books available in all the world's psychiatric libraries about men like Peter Coy Booker. Bloodlines. Poverty. Tough climb. Financial success followed by the masking of what he was. But Con Duggan knew that Peter Booker went far beyond what he was or what a shrink would say he was. He couldn't hide his past. It was smoothed over a bit by his wealth. But he hadn't changed. He had only gotten worse. What he had been made him rich, and remaining true to his past would only make him richer. All else was surface fluff. Peter Coy Booker was a homocidal psychopath and the single most purely evil human being Con had ever encountered.

Their guide led them down a spiral carpeted staircase and into a crystal-chandeliered dining room with a rich, paneled wall covered entirely with paintings of women and sailing ships. A round table had place settings for six, but only Booker was at his chair. The paneled room was otherwise empty except for a tuxedoed steward, nearly invisible against a door that obviously led to the galley. Booker was wearing a dark, expensive-looking suit and a perfectly knotted red power tie. He looked like any banker you might meet in any dining room in the world. He did not get up, just waved Con and Steven to chairs that were pulled out for them by the silent tuxedoed servant. Their seats were across from each other, with places set between theirs and Booker's apparently for guests who would appear later.

"Well, mate, what brings you to this small, insignificant port in the storm, eh? You're looking very well, Con, I might add. For you, I mean.''

"I came to look at a Mosquito. My young friend here is an aircraft engineer. Hawkinge Air Base is only an hour from here. So here I, we, are. I'm here to buy a Mosquito.''

"A bug?''

"No, an airplane. WWII. You remember World War II, Booker. The only recent conflict you didn't personally profit from.''

"Oh, but I did. Came to Chicago. Of course, you knew that. He knows everything about me. Don't you, Con Duggan? Now who or what is this young red-headed gent? Truthfully, I mean. He just doesn't look like an aircraft engineer to me.''

"Steven Dye, designer of weapons for the future and would-be adventurer, meet his bad highness, Peter Coy Booker, thief.''

"Better. Yes, much better. Truth in advertising. I like that. How do you do, Steven Dye.'' Booker got up and walked to Steven's chair, extending his hand. Steven took it and was surprised by its firm grip, its warmth, its . . . its . . . sincerity.

"I do what I'm told, mostly. It's hard to do a lot else around Mr. Duggan.''

"Ah, just so! It must be. A formidable Yank, this one. I know. He's been an irritant to me in international pistol matches.''

"I haven't been an irritant, Booker. I've kicked your ass in every match we ever faced off in.'' Con's eyes were glacial.

"Well, that is true, I suppose. Yes. True. But then, those matches have rules and regulations. I play all contests better when the rules are my own, or at least it's possible to cheat.''

Steven Dye was caught immediately by the tenor of the conversation between the two men. Hatred. Mutual, unhidden hatred blanketed them like an invisible shroud. Somebody clearly was going to get killed here.

"You two don't like each other much, do you?" It was less a question than an obvious fact.

"Like? Well, I'm not at all sure I *like* Con, but I must say, he provides me with considerable sport. Has he told you about any of our earlier, less structured meetings? Probably not . . . Earl, give these men a drink. Where are my manners?"

Earl, the invisible man, took their drink requests and reappeared almost instantly, while the three men said nothing, just letting the tension and heat grow of its own accord. Steven Dye, young and stupid, pushed on after tossing back two ounces of icy vodka. Con Duggan sipped at a pint of Whatleys.

"No, he hasn't. He's told me a bit about your pistol matches. Nothing else too stimulating, I'm afraid. He wants me to design a weapon system for his Mosquito. That's about all I know about him."

"Really? Maggie, do you know about Maggie?"

"His wife, I think. Alaska."

"Wife? Well, I suppose you could call her that, couldn't you, Con? Beautiful woman, that one! She accompanies Con on his biannual pistol matches around the bloody world. I bring ten, he brings Maggie. What she sees in him, I can't imagine."

"That's enough about Maggie, Booker, unless you want me to start breaking all this expensive monogrammed china, along with your expensive head."

For the briefest moment, Steven Dye thought the two men would leap simultaneously at each other's throats. But he sensed they were like wild bulls, probing, pushing. But not yet ready or sure of what territory to defend.

"Well, fine, mate. I only meant she suited you. Not me, but you. There have been other times, other women. Oh, Con and I have fucked a large population of Southeast Asian whores together. We were, at one time, reluctant allies. I was an independent businessman most of the time. Con, of course, was a heroic vision of U.S. interests as embodied by the Marine Corps. He was a sniper. Did you know that? Oh. More vodka? Earl, more vodka for our young friend.'' The vodka appeared, and Steven, noticing Con had scarcely touched his pint of beer, took only a polite sip this time.

"There was one woman I recall in particular. Beautiful even by my rather extreme standards. She once sat completely still in a small box for seven days without food. Just to kill a Marine colonel. She did it, too. She wouldn't let me fuck her. Of course, I could have forced her, but instead I killed her.''

Steven's eyes widened, and he took a gulp of his vodka. This was his first ''black'' mission, and therefore his first encounter with the type of men they would be expected to target.

"Oh, I'm sorry. I don't mean I actually killed her. Con Duggan *killed* her, along with her daughter. No matter. Asiatics have been slaughtering girl babies for centuries. And by then, Con Duggan had certainly gone bloody Asiatic, eh, mate?''

Steven Dye looked at Con Duggan and then at Peter Booker. Now. Surely, right now, death sat to dinner. The two men's eyes locked, and they seemed to strain forward in their chairs.

"I gave her to him, you see. Told him where she was. Boom! One dead gook, one dead gook child. Con left the country after that, I believe. One hundred, wasn't it? Bloody lot of bodies to leave about, wasn't it? Still, if a man has a talent, he ought to use it, whether it be outdoor cooking on the barby or murder. Don't you agree, Mr. Dye?'' Finally, Peter Coy Booker ended his merciless plundering of Con's memory and spoke to Steven, breaking eye contact and, Steven was sure, avoiding final combat.

"Do you like women, Mr. Dye? Pretty women?''

"Sure. Hell, yes.'' Steven had been holding his breath.

"Good. I know Mr. Duggan does. And I have arranged for you to have dinner companions. Earl, bring the ladies, will you?''

A side panel in the wall opened, and three of the most beautiful women Steven Dye had ever seen entered the room. A blonde with a fixed smile and a startling body supporting the tightest sheath dress possible moved to Steven's side and took the chair next to him. When she sat down, the front of her dress parted, showing gartered legs that matched the rest of her. A cool, elegant brunette, draped in a full length, clinging black gown moved to sit next to Con, a slight look of distaste curling the corners of her lovely mouth.

The third woman wore only high heels and a collar around her neck studded with diamonds. Her hands were cuffed in front of her, hiding tiny breasts. She walked to Booker's chair and knelt at his side, an eager look, a look of hope, on her face. Somehow, incongruous as it all was, Con Duggan looked as if this little act of sexual theater was perfectly normal.

"You haven't changed at all, Booker. They are still beautiful, still slightly weird, but by now, I'm unshockable. I like mine, but you know I do, don't you?"

"Yeah. I told her you were in love and wouldn't beat her, which, by the way, she likes. She was brassed-off for a bit, but I begged her to at least eat with us. She will enjoy her meal a lot more, however, if you hit her once or twice."

"I'll think about it."

Astonished, Steven Dye watched as Con Duggan gave Booker what looked like a genuine smile. Jesus Christ! When did the white rabbit show up? The brunette smiled up at Con, anticipating a possible beating which apparently would make her happy.

The blonde with Steven Dye had placed one slim hand on his crotch and the other on his knee, while giving him what he could only describe later, much later, as a glazed look of complete, utter need.

"She'll probably be under the table and in your lap in a moment. Sick girl, that one. Pretty, though, don't you agree? Now, mates, what will you have? Fish, fowl, or meat? Speak up now, I'm starved, and on my bloody boat, when I'm bloody starved, my bloody guests eat!"

• • •

The blonde was under the table for the third time in an hour, once again trying to earn her keep as decided by their host, the bad Mr. Booker. Each time he had pushed her away, and she had returned to her chair, picking at her dinner.

Con Duggan seemed to be enjoying himself, chewing lustily on a two-inch-thick steak large enough to raft a family of gerbils across the Atlantic. The brunette's slim hands waved in exquisite, feminine movements as she gestured, talking in broken French and fractured English about the joys of female submission. Con Duggan would not do what the sleek vibrating little woman wanted, but he was impressed nevertheless. Booker knew and had provided something to completely distract and entertain him. Booker needed to manipulate his enemies. In this case, it appeared he had been successful.

Finally the women were banished by a wave of Booker's hand, much to the disappointment of Con's semi-linguistic, elegant pervert, who told him as she waved her lace garter belt over her head that he was clearly unworthy of her and had no idea what he was missing. Con agreed with apparent good humor. Steven Dye's blonde had not protested, and Steven could not look her in the eye. It wouldn't have mattered, because there was nothing to see in her eyes anyway. The naked girl in handcuffs simply followed the other two out.

"Come, mates, let's leave the dishes, shall we? Follow me." The two team members followed Booker down the hall to a very masculine, very tastefully done study. They each took a cigar, a brandy, and settled back into comfortable leather chairs.

"Well now, Con Duggan and Steven Dye, I'm here in England to display my models and my model-building capabilities. Tell me, why are you here?"

Con Duggan watched his demented host while he searched his own mind for an answer Booker would believe. When he spoke, Booker believed him.

•

"I came to England to stop your latest business venture, Booker."

Steven Dye jumped in his seat and nearly spilled his brandy. Booker looked at Con with astonishment then quickly extinguished it from his eyes.

"Have you now? And what business venture is that, mate? Surely my models are of no threat to the common good."

"The Brits think you're about to kill their Prime Minister, with the frog President thrown in. So they asked my help, sort of for old times' sake."

"Bloody wild, Duggan! Surely you don't think a man in my position would be involved in anything so farfetched! Glory, mate, you've really jumped your pouch!"

"That's what I told them, Booker. You're already rich as you can be. Then I thought about it a bit more. And the more I thought about it, the more I was sure you would try it. The whole scheme is just wild and woolly enough for a gentleman sheep herder from Australia. Running guns and drugs is profitable enough I'm sure, but there can't be much of an edge to it for you anymore. You've bought most of the drug enforcement people you need, and you've murdered the ones you don't need or couldn't buy."

"Really? Please go on, Duggan. Fascinating stuff, don't you think, Mr. Dye?"

"Oh, yeah, fascinating. He's crazy, you know. So I don't pay much attention to what he says." Steven thought Con had perhaps actually gone crazy. Here he was, telling the bad buy how bad he was. It seemed a bit outside what he thought good spies and secret agents did. He'd seen movies. James Bond would never do this.

Con sipped his brandy, a smile on his face, but not in his eyes. "Booker, what really have you done lately? Made more money, bought more people, bought more things. That's not enough for you anymore. You need to make a big splash in the sewer you float around in so all the other rats will recognize who the really big rodent is.

This deal would be worth a lot of money, I'm sure. But it's what it will bring you down the road that's important to you. How or why you thought nobody would pick up on this, I can't figure. Did you just think you might sail in here, do this simple little hit, and sail out?"

"*If* I were actually involved in this charade, and mind you, I'm not saying I am, I should have been thoroughly dissuaded this morning. The local intelligence agencies seem to be here in force, a fact they demonstrated to me and my comrades when I went ashore. A bit heavy-handed, but I got the point. They seemed determined to monitor my behavior. So you might just as well go back to your Mosquito hunt, if there really is one at Hawkinge. Because I'm not likely to be allowed to venture far without the accompaniment of MI-5 and MI-6 and the CIA and whoever else might be interested. The exhibition lasts just two days. When it's over, I shall pack up my miniature armies and slide gracefully out to sea. Now then, Duggan, you and your 'engineer' friend will have to forgive me. I have a lot to do." Booker touched a button on his chair, and a crewmember appeared in the doorway. Booker stood up and extended his hand to Steven, who hesitated, scrambling to switch his brandy snifter and his cigar from his right hand to his left. Finally freed, he took Booker's hand. This time, he detected no sincerity at all. Booker's eyes were empty of expression, but he held his body in a tight, tense crouch, a sort of combat handshake.

"I would offer you my hand as well, old Con, but you wouldn't take it now, would you?"

"No. Not now, Booker."

"Well then. Perhaps we will meet next year. The Steel Challenge in Arizona. Or the Bianchi Cup. You do still *compete*, now? I mean, have you tossed in your guns?"

"No, Booker. I still have my guns."

"He's quite a shot, Mr. Dye. Did you know that?"

"I've heard. Yes."

"And you, Mr. Dye. Are you quite a shot as well?"

"Nope. I just design them. I don't shoot at all."

"Bloody good sport, shooting." Booker turned his back on the two men without another word. The crewman escorted them to the waiting Zodiac, and they were quickly ferried back across the harbor to Folkstone. A brief walk, and they were back at their hotel suite as well. Steven looked out across the harbor at the *Stingray* glittering in the cold night, big and sleek and somehow overwhelmingly evil. He and Con had hardly spoken since leaving the yacht. It had been the strangest night of his young life. Bad guy. Yachts. And fear. A lot of that. If Steven Dye had been a virgin at 6:00 P.M., he was a popped cherry in the intelligence business now.

"Tomorrow morning—this morning—we have to find a place to shoot the bad guys, and we have to locate them all as well."

"We'll shoot if they show up, right?"

"No, Mr. Dye. We are going to hit the slick Mr. Booker a day early. Maybe we won't tell the Brits about it either."

"You mean the day *before* the ceremony."

"Why not?"

"No reason, I guess." Steven Dye, the youngest and newest agent on the team, kept his mouth shut. But he could think of plenty of reasons. After the light went out, it took him two hours to get to sleep. When he finally slept, he had a dream about a large white boat with a bright red mouth running him over and swallowing him up.

"He don't seem like bloody much to me." Dorsey was sitting a few feet away from Booker, cleaning and re-cleaning an old beat-up Uzi, one of his personal favorites. Weapons. What would he be without them?

"He doesn't, eh? Well, he is bloody much. Steven Dye is new. I want you to hit him. It will be easier, and it will send the message I want to deliver to good old Duggan."

"Whyn't you hit the Duggan bloke? I can handle him."

"No, you can't. Besides, I like him around. When the

day comes, I'll kill him myself. And we are not staying past our exhibition's time to be here. We're leaving in two days."

"But we have a contract. We should . . ."

"Dorsey?"

"Yeah?"

"Shut the bloody fuck up!"

"Well, if it's to be that way, then all right."

"Good. But hit the young one. And do it neatly, will you?"

"Neatly. Right then. I'm to off the bugger neatly. No mess then, right?"

"No mess, Dorsey. It should be easy. He's only a boy, after all."

7

Con Duggan and Steven Dye crossed Folkstone's Bouvier Square and walked into the offices of the East Kent Road Car Company, Ltd. Steven had no idea what Con had in mind. He thought they were looking for a shooting platform, a hotel, a church, a high point. He was right, of course.

"Good morning, sir. How may I be of service?" The East Kent Road Car Company, Ltd. had a very dazzling representative in its offices. Twenty-two. Busty. A red slash for a mouth. Black hair, short skirt, flirty eyes. Steven Dye made a mental note to come back, assuming, of course, he didn't get real dead here in the Mother Country.

"We'd like some information about buses." The bus lady gave Con Duggan a once over and calculated his age. Determining she was too young for him, she turned her considerable charms on Steven Dye. She leaned for-

ward and her skirt rode higher up the back of her thighs.
England seemed to be populated by young women with
very long legs and not enough material in their skirts.

"Tell me, just what kind of information would you
like?" She looked right past Con.

"Your home phone number would do." Steven caught
her look and gave her one of his own.

Blushing coquettishly, she said, "You! Well, I mean
now, you're a Yank now, aren't you, love? You Yanks!"
She gave Steven Dye a hip roll to match her eyes. A
flushed cheek and a calculated sigh followed, meant to
lift her considerable breasts and young Steven Dye's
ardor.

"And I thought we won the revolution." Con Duggan
gave his teammate . . . teammate, well, yes, he was that
. . . a droll smile.

The bus company gave him another look, interest this
time, but . . . "You're the cheeky pair, aren't you just."
Her breasts jumped under her uniform. Cheeky. Well . . .
she was bouncy, at least.

"We would like to hire a bus. A double-decker bus.
How much might that . . . cost us?" Con Duggan gave
Steven a meaningful glance, the look of a friend in a soda
shop, handing a girl off between them like a football.

"Well, do you have a large party?" With this comment, she gave Steven a look guaranteed to incite. Soon,
thought Con, her nostrils would start to flare.

"Yes. We have a large party. My young friend with
the red hair and dashing manner and me. Two. That is our
party. And we expect to drive the bus ourselves."

"Drive it yourselves? Well, you can't do that, I can tell
you right now! You must have a company driver. Or . . .
or a substitute, but trained driver." Her look got more
meaningful than ever. Steven Dye picked up the ball and
ran with it.

"Do you . . . ah . . . know a trained, substitute driver?"

"Well, I'm trained to drive. But I'm only allowed to
drive off season. . . . Oh, it is off season, isn't it? Oh.
Well." She turned bright red and actually lowered her

eyes. Con Duggan moved to make this deal, while it was still a deal to be made.

"How much for the bus, and of course you as the driver? Would one thousand pounds cover it? Two? Three, perhaps?"

She was no virgin. "Yes, three, I think. When do you need it? With me driving, of course. I'm free of the office today at sixish. For three days. Three thousand *per day* would do it, I'm sure." She gave Con a look of real challenge. There was more to this girl than he'd thought.

"Per day . . . three per day. My, what a big girl you are." Con Duggan turned to his horny young partner. "Steven, I expect you to handle this. Have the young . . . lady at the Langhorne Gardens in the morning with her bus. I suggest you write it up as a party of 40, World War II vets, here to visit Hawkinge Museum. We will need the bus for 48 hours, beginning tomorrow. Is that within your authority, Miss . . . Miss . . . ?"

"James. Penelope James. And it *is* Miss. I mean, I'm not married." She gave Steven Dye a mournful, female look.

"Well, Miss James. I shall leave you with my young friend. Steven Dye, USA, meet Miss Penelope James, United Kingdom. Good night to you both."

Con Duggan walked out of the East Kent Road Car Company assured of a double decker bus. A shooting platform with two floors driven by a busty daughter of Old England.

Con spent the day walking Folkstone's twisting water-front streets. The day was bitter cold with a brisk wind cutting across the channel and blowing inland. Even in the afternoon, it seemed nearly dark by two. Con felt a strange dread, a persistent feeling that he wasn't on top of things. It had been a very long time, after all, since he'd hunted human targets. Part of him wanted to board a commercial jet and kiss this operation goodbye. He needed Maggie. God, what a revelation that had been. He missed her, and he needed her. A man could have a woman like Maggie and never realize he had a treasure. But Con realized it. As he walked, he began to identify agents and shooters of all kinds, out of place by their dress or their attitude or their wayward eyes.

"Mr. Duggan?"

He was jerked from his reverie by the melodious voice of the lovely Madeline, she of the new brand of agents who liked to lay down on the job, so to speak.

"Hello, there. Are you following me?" She put her arm through his and walked with him, a gray-haired old guy with a knockout English "bird" window-shopping on his credit card. Or so it appeared if you were inclined to look.

"Don't be silly, Mr. Duggan. Why on earth would I follow you?"

"Because you like the cut of my jib?"

"Oh, yes, I do, actually. But I've been asked by your Mr. Barns to look you up. He will be here about four, and he wants to see you. He will meet you at the Folkstone Race Track. He asked me to tell you he'd brought you something or other, but he wouldn't say what."

"Didn't you ask?"

"Of course not. What do you think I am, a snoop?" She looked up at him, trim and vital and sexy, and she was as dangerous as they come.

"Where, by the way, is Mr. Dye? I'd like to . . . to see him."

"I'll let him know. At the moment, he's waiting for a bus."

"Really. A bus, is it? That's a new one, I must say. I'll have to leave you now. Do keep that appointment at the racetrack."

"Sure. I'll be there."

"Right. I'm off." She stood on her tiptoes and brushed his throat with her lips before moving briskly down the street, her legs flashing in the gray afternoon, miniskirted in spite of the cold. At the end of the block, she turned back toward him, waved, and climbed into the back seat of a waiting sedan. A faint trace of her perfume wafted about him, and he could feel the warmth of her lips on his neck. Young women. They were terrific. His day brightened, and his dark thoughts dissipated.

Folkstone Race Course

"Nice country track." said Michael.

"Yeah. Small, but nice. Why did you want to meet me here?"

"Quiet. Empty. Safe." Michael gave Con a tired smile.

"Good reasons."

"Yup."

"So?"

"The SIKIM is in the van. I wondered what the hell you wanted me to do with it."

"I rented a bus. A double-decker bus." Con waited for the explosion.

But Michael just said, "For the SIKIM?"

"Why not? We can mount it and move it around. I've decided to hit Booker a day early. Tomorrow night, late. After midnight."

"You can't do that, Con. What about the British?"

"What about them?" Con was leaning against the white metal track rail smoking a cigarette, his eyes lidded and distant.

"Well, we can't just go off on our own." Michael sucked at his lower lip with his teeth. He looked worried and tense.

"Sure we can. That's what they want us to do. I'm just suggesting we do it a day early, that's all. I was out on his boat last night. I want to kill him. And soon, before he leaves. I told him why I was here."

"*You what?*"

"I told him why I was here because he asked me, and because he knew anyway. He always knows. He likes it this way. And he will leave the dignitaries alone now. He'll take the money and just leave."

"Booker never just leaves, Con, you know that.

You've given him pretty good reason to kill you for the hell of it.''

"Yes, I have. But he won't kill me. I'll kill him.''

Michael Barns studied Con's face. He saw nothing except the reason he'd pulled his old friend back into the shooting business. Con had on his shooter's face. He was in the hunt. He would either have to allow Con to do it his way or pack up and go home. And that would mean the unit had failed. He could not allow the unit to fail in its first mission. The mission was the most important thing. Stop Peter Coy Booker from executing his plan. What difference did it make how it was done? Results were what Michael had to deliver. A safe Prime Minister, a safe French President, and if possible, a bad-guy body count for the Senate Committees on Intelligence and Foreign Affairs to brag about. What the hell, that's what mattered, wasn't it? For a brief instant, he thought about Maggie, but he brushed his feelings aside. Con would be okay. Sure he would. Con was always okay.

"Just keep me informed. I set up a shoot team with radios and five cars at the Gresham Hotel. I'll leave the van with them for security. The British don't know anything about the SIKIM-1000.''

"Really, Michael? Why not?''

"Hell, it might not work, you know.''

"I hadn't thought of that. Mr. Dye says it will work, so I think it will.''

"Fine. Let's hope so. What do you intend to do with it?''

"I'm not exactly sure, Michael. But we'll think of something.''

"I'm sure you will, Con. By the way, you have lipstick on your neck.''

"I know. I'm having a hell of a good time for a poor old ex-Marine grunt. Thanks for the invite, Michael.''

"Thank me later when I know I did you a favor.'' Michael Barns walked off before he could change his mind and stop this insanity. He drove the van to the Gresham Hotel and settled in to monitor his team. Very soon, much sooner than he had expected, people were going to die in large numbers in the quaint old city of Folkstone, England.

La Parisienne Night Club was advertised as the UK's first "Eurotèque," a title used to describe a very noisy place with bright flashing lights. But it was a perfect place for Miss Penelope James to take her Yank. Steven Dye, whip slim and dressed in an expensive black silk shirt and tight black slacks, loved to dance. Fast. Slow. Hands on or hands off. And he was very good at it.

Penelope, having cinched the bus deal and the nine thousand pounds that went with it, was in a partying mood. She was dressed in a flaming red mini-skirt, gartered thigh-high red boots, and a top just barely within the laws of decency.

The place was jammed, and the dancers were dripping with hormonal excess. Steven Dye, less than twenty-four hours after his exotic dinner, was beginning to like what he did more than he would have imagined.

Penelope, dancing away from him, spun around and looked over her shoulder at him, her hips grinding to the music. He noticed she had *very* tiny panties on, not much more than a G-string. She stood, turned, and feet planted, aimed her pelvis at him, in time to the music, of course. Sweat glistened at her exposed neck, the fullness and freedom of her breasts apparent to anyone who wanted to look. Steven Dye was mesmerized.

They had walked in, she in front as they entered, knowing she had a . . . distinctive walk. The music had just begun, and she pulled him right onto the dance floor. They danced the entire set, and when the music finally stopped, they clung to each other briefly before finding a table to sit and rest, though at their ages, they recovered very quickly. Her eyes danced with excitement, her hand warm and moist as she leaned forward to accept a light for her cigarette.

"Oh, Yank, I just love it here! It's so excit'n, don't you think? The lights and all, the music, the drinks, the men!

Did you ever see such moist male flesh in your life? Sandra, she's my cousin, she gets all sorts of fellas out of here. She's not easy, mind you, but she does have her weakness, you see. Men, I mean. Sometimes, when she stays at my flat, and it's a bloody *little*, tiny flat, I'll tell you, she and her boy-friends have at it in the next bed! Drives me out of my knickers! All that panting! Oh . . . I do run on, don't I, Yank?''

"Steven. Please call me Steven."

"Well, of course I will! It's just that sometimes when I'm very excited or happy or scared, I just talk on and on. My mum, bless her departed soul, used to think I was a bit unstable that way, but I only do it when I'm happy or whatever. When I was only a little girl, I'd pee my knickers, but of course, I'm not little anymore, am I, Steven?''

"Well, you sure do . . ."

"Yes. I know what you mean. I had *no* titties until I was fourteen, and then, all of a summer, I had these. Do you like them? Oh, I hope so. I love to have them touched a lot. Sucked, actually. Promise me you will always touch them. Oh. The music is back. C'mon, Steven, Yank, let's dance.''

"Well, I, maybe we should—"

"Dance with me, Steven Dye. It's a slow dance, and you'll have to hold me close. Come, Yank. Hold me and we'll take each other's measure, if you know what I mean, and I'm sure you don't.''

The music was slow, a bluesy, low-down song heavy on the bass and drums. Penelope put her arms around his neck and pressed her body against his. He could feel her pubic mound fitted against his. He was in a state of complete horniness, his hard-on fitted to her body like a hotdog to a bun. She buried her face in his throat, and they stood in one place, flat against each other while a hundred other couples pressed against them in a mass of sexual energy leashed only by its public happening. She put her mouth to his ear, her hips moving in little jerky circles against his hard-on.

"Oh, Steven, can you hear it?"

"What?" She seemed to be vibrating in his arms. He couldn't back away because of the crowd. But he wouldn't have anyway.

She held him fiercely to her, her hips suddenly still, her thighs trembling against his. Her mouth against his ear felt hot and dry. Love potion, that's what she was. A walking, talking love potion. The slow dance ended, and they walked dazedly back to their table, sat down and just looked at each other. For the moment, Penelope had nothing at all to say. Across the room, Dorsey and three men watched the pair with more than a little interest.

Langhorne Gardens Hotel
Folkstone, England

Con Duggan held the phone cupped to his ear so he could hear Maggie's voice, her image clear in his mind, the smell of her, the softness, the round softness he missed and worried he might never see or touch again.

"How ya doin', old man?"

"Fine. The weather's cold, so I feel sort of at home. Alaska was never this cold, though. English cold has an attitude problem. Goes right through you."

For a moment Maggie did not reply. When she did, it was as if she was in the suite with him. "I miss you, baby. I want a lot more of what I got in Las Vegas."

"Really? I remember. Pretty good for a couple of old folks."

"Speak for yourself, Duggan!" He could see her, the phone pressed to her ear, twisting her long black tresses into knots while she talked, her voice transmitting a mock reprimand across the Atlantic.

"I meant pretty good, considering you are in love with a doddering old fool, Maggie."

"True. You do dodder, don't you? Con, are you okay? Is all going well?"

"Sure it is. No big deal here. Just snoopin' around in the bushes."

"You're very good in the bushes, Con. Remember at the lakeshore last summer?"

Oh, yes, he remembered. Her naked body emerging from the icy blue-green of the lake, tossing her hair in a shower of spray, her eyes hot in the sun, falling to her knees at his feet and sucking him into her mouth, wrapping her hair around him, gripping him with her hair, and . . .

"Yeah, Mags, I remember. But I'd rather not, since I can't reach you at the moment."

"Good! I want you to remember. When I think about you, I—" There was a loud knock at his door, and Con broke into his increasingly erotic conversation with Maggie to answer it.

"Wait one, honey. Somebody at the door."

Con crossed the room and opened the door, something he would not have done without checking who it might have been if he'd not been distracted by Maggie's phone sex.

"Well, Mr. Duggan, may I come in? Your Mr. Dye is in a bit of trouble, I believe." Tiptoes again, a kiss on his neck, and Madeline brushed past him and into the suite, sitting on the bed and digging in her purse for a cigarette. "Tell me, Con, have you a light for a wayward spy?"

For a moment Con had no idea what to do. He tossed his lighter to Madeline and picked up the phone.

"You're a dear, Con. Thanks ever so." Madeline clicked the Zippo and tossed it back to Con. Maggie, thousands of miles away, heard every word.

" 'Oh, thanks ever so' . . . really, Con, what are you doing?"

"Oh. It's just . . . business. I mean, Madeline is a . . . well, she's a . . ."

"Can I make myself comfortable, Con?" Madeline, attired in blue jeans and a leather coat, looked anything but sexy. With a mischievous grin, she lowered her voice an octave. "Scotch, Con, or vodka?" She put her fingers over her lovely mouth to suppress a grin.

"Scotch? Vodka? Con Duggan, who is that woman I hear? Con Duggan, you'd better explain pretty damn quick!"

"Maggie, honey, it's nothing, I swear! Madeline's just trying to be funny, that's all."

"Oh, is she now?"

"Yes. She's . . ."

"Con, I'm going to shower now. Don't go away." Madeline, after saying this as loudly as she could, rolled over on the bed and covered her laughter with a pillow.

"Con Duggan, you call me later if you can get the British out of your bedroom!" The transatlantic line went dead.

"Terrific, Madeline. The love of my life just hung up on me."

"Perhaps she's not the love of your life."

"Yes, she is."

"Well. Right, then. Now I suggest we go dancing."

"I don't dance."

"You can learn. Mr. Steven Dye is currently with a nearly naked woman at the disco."

"That would be the bus company."

"I beg your pardon?"

"Like I said earlier today. He was waiting for a bus."

"Oh, quite. Apparently, she was the 'bus' you meant."

"No. The bus is real. Two decker. She's going to drive it for us. Three thousand pounds a day."

"Three thousand!"

"Three thousand. Three days." Her eyebrow arched critically.

"I'm in the wrong line of work, Con. Nevertheless, the young lovers are at peril, to put it mildly. Dorsey and three of his cronies are also at the disco."

"Dorsey?" Con had no idea whom she meant.

"Peter Booker's number-one man."

"C'mon, Madeline, let's go to the dance." Con grabbed Madeline by the hand and pulled her out the door after him. As the door shut behind them, his hotel suite phone began to ring. But the next time Maggie spoke to Con Duggan wouldn't be sexy—or funny.

"You're terribly big for such a slim, tallish fella, did you know that?" Penelope was still flushed and Steven was even more so.

"I'm sorry?"

"Big. Down there. You know." She waggled her slim fingers in the direction of his crotch.

"I am? I had no idea. Do you have a lot to compare me with?"

"Oh, just oodles. I lost my cherry to a banker's son at age fifteen. Said he'd marry me. He didn't mean it, of course. Men never mean what they say. Me mum told me that, and she ought to have known, because she was married four times."

"Four?"

"Would have been five, but she took sick and died two weeks before the fifth marriage date. Bad sort of a bloke anyway."

"I'm sorry. I mean, about your mother."

"Don't be. She never had a happy time of life. Better off, my auntie says.'Course, my auntie's married to a vicar and probably never had sex with the lights on."

"Do you always talk this way?"

"About sex, you mean? Well, I like sex. I write poetry about sexy things. I've done one called 'Multiple Orgasms.' It's lovely, I think. I'll let you read it one day after we've known each other longer." Penelope gave him a merry little smile and kicked her chair around the table next to his. Her fingers found him and she began to kiss his ear. He wondered what she did with men she really liked.

• • •

Dorsey watched Steven Dye dance for two hours. He watched the couple grow more and more animated and enamored with each other. Finally, they stopped dancing altogether and just sat and stared into each other's eyes. He nodded knowingly at his tablemates. It would be easy, and considering the little doxie liked sex so much and seemed to be dressed for it, it looked like it might be a lot of fun as well.

"Why don't we go to my flat, Yank, and you can tell me all about the United States of America, and I'll tell you all about Birmingham."

"We have a Birmingham. It's in Alabama."

"Do you? Oh, goody! I'll show you my Birmingham if you'll show me yours." Her slim hand came to rest on his cheek in a touch so intimate he felt weak.

"Right. I'll show you mine, you show me yours." He stood up, aware of his body in relation to hers, and guided her through the crowd. They picked up their coats, and she pushed her buttocks against him as she slipped into hers, her head back, her lips brushing lightly against his cheeks. He'd never been so shakingly horny in his life.

"And I have one to show you that you'll never forget." Saying that, she kissed him ferociously and pulled him toward the exit and out of the disco.

It was very cold, and a thick fog had descended on Folkstone, a swirly, spooky fog right out of a black-and-white horror movie from the past. Steven's leather jacket was very stylish, but it was also useless against the thick fog. His ardor cooled with the weather.

"Oh, my. It's gone, hasn't it?" She had him by the crotch, her hand moving with slow but deliberate urgency.

"No. It's just cold. Now, where is this flat?"

"Well, c'mon then, it's only a little way. And it's quite warm there. My landlord is a fat old man who reads dirty mags and such, but he always makes sure my flat is warm."

"Good. That's what I need. Something soft and round in something warm and flat."

"Oh, you Yanks! You're a poet at heart!"

She took his hand and began to walk, her spike heels clicking on the sidewalk as they headed away from the brightly lit disco. After a block or so, she stopped and kissed him fiercely, right in the middle of the road. She took his hand and placed it under her skirt. She was radiating heat that seemed to brush away the fog. She ground herself against his hand, spreading her legs to allow him access.

"Oh, I'm so hot. Put your fingers in me, and you'll see. Oh, Yank, I think . . ." And then she was jerked away from him, and he was held by the arms and then knocked to the ground by a blow to the back that temporarily paralyzed him. He heard her cry out, followed by the clatter of one of her heels as she was dragged off the street into an alley, and he was propelled forward by three men who half-carried and half-pushed him after her.

"Well now, what have we here? A pretty girl, unescorted on the dark streets of England? Mr. Dye, you are going to have a very short stay in England. Mr. Booker believes you've already worn out your welcome. So he sent me to escort you off. Way off. And the trixie miss here, well, we'll just bugger her until she quiets down."

Penelope was straining against Dorsey, trying to escape, her face showing more determination than terror. Steven was filled with guilt and admiration for her, mixed with the real fear that he was about to die.

Dorsey spun Penelope around and ripped her top off with his hand, pulling her toward him, trying to kiss her breasts. Steven struggled to reach her, but could not get away. He watched helplessly as Dorsey pushed Penelope to the ground and jerked her skirt up as he freed his engorged penis from his pants. Penelope waited, arms over her chest, legs spread, until Dorsey started to get down to the ground. Then a high-heeled foot lashed out and caught her tormentor right in the crotch.

He clutched himself with one hand and yelped in pain.

Even in the fog, Steven Dye could see the triumphant look on Penelope's face. She tried to kick him again and reached up to scratch his face. Dorsey, bellowing like a wounded bull, lashed out with his fist, knocking her back and stopping her resistance. Rhythmically, he slapped her face from side to side until finally she lay still, all the fight gone out of her.

Dorsey pulled a long thin knife from his boot and settled the blade against her breast. She lay completely still, her breath loud in the stillness of the alley.

"Go ahead, you slimy bastard. But you'll get no pleasure from it!"

The fog-shrouded stillness was abruptly broken by a man and woman singing at the top of their lungs, a drunken pair coming down the long curve of the alley. Dorsey pulled Penelope to her feet, the knife at her throat. She was too frightened to struggle.

"Don't talk now, pretty one. We'll just wait till the charming couple pass, and if you behave, it won't go so hard on you." The three men holding Steven Dye put him up against the cool, uneven brick wall of a hundred-year-old building. Afraid for Penelope, he said nothing, his mind racing ahead, searching for a plan, just any fucking way out of this cold, damp hell he'd found himself in.

The man and woman came on down the alley, clutching each other, weaving back and forth, bumping into the narrow walls of the alley. They were still singing, words he knew but couldn't place, a song everybody knew, a song . . . It was "Yankee Doodle." And then the couple separated, the man leaping at Dorsey, the woman suddenly very stiff and still, arms outstretched, the gun silenced but winking brightly through the fog. Steven's human handcuffs fell away as the gun winked on, following the two men down, three slugs for each, rolling them away like bad sausage with broken casings, their blood and guts all over the alley.

Steven spun around, taking the third man down with him, locking his hands around the man's throat, sitting on him, choking him with a strength he didn't know he possessed, until the man, who weighed 250 pounds, threw him off and reversed their positions, now choking Steven. The fog brightened again as Madeline's gun lit up the alley once more, sending four bullets into the hulk holding Steven in a death grip at the neck. The man grunted, falling away from Steven like a busted sack of produce. Steven scrambled to his feet, saw Penelope held by the shoulders, a knife at her throat, and Con Duggan, a thin line of blood on his cheek, his body tense, only three feet from Dorsey and his captive. The sudden assault had only partially worked. His assailants were dead. Madeline had blown them away. But Con Duggan's rush had failed. He'd been cut, and Dorsey still had Penelope. The fog thickened, chilling Steven to the bone. Three dead in less time than it takes to say it. Steven had no idea what to do. This was not shooting. This was something else entirely.

Then Duggan spoke. "You must be Dorsey, although I was told by my friend with the large gun in her hand that you were Booker's number-one man, and I find that hard to believe. He would never have let an asshole like you work for him when I first met him. Let her go, and I won't cut your nuts off with your own knife." Con's voice had a chilling, hard edge.

"Big talk, mate, but I have the knife and a doxie throat to cut with it!"

Madeline was standing statue-like in the middle of the street forty feet from Dorsey and his captive, her legs braced, ready to shoot. Con Duggan looked behind him and glanced at Steven.

"You okay?"

"Fine. I'm fine. Just like the cavalry. I'm rescued."

Con turned back to deal with his remaining problem. "Let her go, Dorsey, and you walk away. If you hurt her, you die. The little lady with the big gun will see to that."

"I'll cut her. I swear I will!"

"Walk away, Dorsey." Madeline had moved closer now. Twenty feet. "Walk away, and I won't splatter what bloody little brain tissue you have all over this street."

"Big talk again. You won't shoot, and I'm taking this little lady with me."

Con's voice lashed out at Dorsey, whip-like and hot. "No, you're not. Go ahead. Cut her throat. I'll wait right here. I don't give a fuck what you do to her. I don't even know the woman." Steven Dye could not believe his ears. Had Con lost his mind? Penelope was an innocent here. What the hell was he doing?

"You don't mean that, Duggan."

"Yes, I do. Go ahead, Dorsey. Cut her throat."

Dorsey, astonished, loosened his grip on Penelope. She burst free, knocking Dorsey to the ground and hurling herself into Steven's arms, her momentum carrying them both to the slick cobblestoned street. She clutched him to her, finally afraid, sobbing uncontrollably.

Madeline fired twice, but missed. Con Duggan landed on Dorsey as he struggled to his feet, pulling his cherished Uzi from its shoulder holster, spraying bullets out and toward the fog-shrouded forms facing him in the alley. But he was too late, and the bullets spattered harmlessly against the walls.

The struggle was brief and fierce. Madeline moved close, her gun waving over the two men as they rolled over and over, silent except for grunts of exertion and explosive bursts of expelled breath accompanied by curses. They came to a halt against an alley wall, Madeline hovering right over them. Steven Dye held the sobbing Penelope to his chest as headlights stabbed their way through the gray fog of the alley. Finally, Con Duggan stood up, shaking his head like a bear over a kill, stumbling back, only Madeline's quick reaction to balance him saving him from a hard fall. On the street, Dorsey lay gasping, his own knife protruding from his chest like a cross over a grave. They stood above him as he tried to talk, his voice choked with blood that spilled from his throat and down his neck. He coughed and tried to get up, pulling at the knife. Madeline fired once, and he lay back, finally dead, a monster that had taken considerable effort to kill.

• • •

The lights from the police cars at both ends of the alley cast eerie, flickering splashes of red and blue through the thick fog, disco lights over a graveyard. Folkstone citizens stood outside the police lines, trying to penetrate the darker depths of the center of the alley. British agents zipped Dorsey and his friends into the back of a government hearse. Steven held Penelope close to him, leaning against a wall, her body covered and warmed by a wool blanket from one of the police cars. She had stopped crying and in fact was watching the entire process with bright, glittering eyes, showing more than a little interest in the whole process.

"That girl has spunk." Madeline, hands in her pockets, shoulders hunched against the cold, nodded her head toward Steven and Penelope.

"Yes. A good thing, too. It might have gone worse. Much worse. You're not short on spunk yourself. Nice shooting. Very nice. You saved the bunch of us. All three of them were carrying weapons."

"Tell me, Duggan, what am I supposed to feel right now? In truth, this is the first time I've ever had to use anything more than a garter belt and knickers in this business. I don't feel much of anything."

"You will. Later. You will feel relief. They are dead and you are alive."

"And that's all?"

"Hopefully. Don't dwell on it, and don't worry about it. But don't get used to it either."

"I won't. That I could never do."

"What now, Maddy?"

"Why don't we go back to the Langhorne Gardens? We can contact Mr. Booker from there. I think he'll move on without much urging, don't you?"

"I don't want him to move on. Clearly he'll do nothing now against the dignitaries. He'll take his money and his not very significant personnel losses, and he'll just sail off. We have to keep him here for forty-eight more hours so I can kill him."

"That is not in the national interest of my government, Con."

"Fuck your government, Maddy. Let's go back to the hotel and talk about this."

"The job as I see it is finished, Con." Maddy, sexy Maddy, suddenly looked like a spinster aunt determined to have no fun.

"No, it's not. When Booker is dead, it's finished. C'mon, Maddy, let's go get warm."

"What about the young woman?"

"My bus driver? Hell, bring her too. She looks like she's having a terrific time."

"This is crazy, Mr. Duggan."

"Sure. I know that. But you'll go along with it anyway."

"Yes, I suppose I will." In minutes the alley was empty of all but damp cobblestones and fog.

The Langhorne Gardens, a classy, respectable hotel, had nevertheless seen its share of bizarre guests. Keeping a stiff, British upper lip was simply done, so when the nearly naked, puffy-faced girl wrapped in a blanket and escorted by an equally disheveled trio walked through the lobby, nothing at all was said. A slight sniff of displeasure from the desk clerk and a whispered, "What do you expect from the Americans?" the only comment to the bellboy. He might have run away in terror if he'd known what they'd just done in the alley less than a mile away and what they were to bring about in less than thirty-six hours.

Penelope, showered and wearing one of Con's turtlenecks and nothing else, sat on the bed and sipped at a glass three-quarters full of Scotch. She was in good spirits, fairly bouncing on the bed with excitement. She'd not stopped talking since she walked completely nude and dripping wet from the shower, shocking the others into a frantic search for something for her to wear. Modesty, she'd told them, was for old fogeys with bad bodies and Canadians, whom she seemed to dislike immensely.

Madeline said, "You know, Con, we really have no more reason to go on with this. As I said, and I'm sure Reggie Farquarson would agree, we should just walk away now."

"That's crazy, Maddy. You admitted the Prime Minister and the French President were never in any real danger. You wanted Booker. Why back away from that now?"

"He will tread very lightly, Con. He will close the Euro-militaire Exhibition and leave. He will provoke nothing."

"Fuck him. We'll provoke *him*. And if that doesn't work out, we'll just hit him anyway. I didn't come this far to just go back home empty. I say we hit him. With or without your help, that is what I intend to do."

"How? What if he simply stays on the boat?"

"Steven can deal with that, can't you, Mr. Dye?"

Steven Dye had been very quiet since they returned to the hotel. He could see very little past the horror in the alley and the hard face that he'd been waylaid by Dorsey and his men because he'd had a hard-on for the sprightly girl sitting next to him wearing Con's shirt. He'd been stupid, and he'd endangered the whole team. He'd not even been competent enough to escape without the help of a woman with a gun working for another country. He owed Madeline his life. Con threw him a lifeline.

"Tell Maddy about the SIKIM-1000, Steven. The Brits don't even know what it is. Michael Barns has it stashed only five minutes away. Tell her what it can do to Booker's fancy boat."

"The SIKIM-1000?" Madeline was caught off guard. Con was right. She had no idea what it was.

"Tell her, Steven."

"It's a weapon. A weapon system. I designed it. It has multiple uses, sights, capabilities. We were going to mount it on a bus, though beyond that I have no idea how Con intended to use it. Penelope was going to drive, and

I don't know how he was going to bring that idea forward either.''

"Well, now he doesn't bloody have to, does he? I'll do it! Whatever it is.'' Penelope was bouncing up and down on the bed, clapping her hands like a delighted child, and freshly scrubbed, if a little bruised, she looked like one too. If you paid no attention to her body, that is. Every time she bounced, Con's shirt rode farther up above her sleek thighs.

"That's bloody impossible! Con, this, this . . . woman can't be involved in this preposterous idea! You intended to allow her to drive you around in a bus while you use this sackthem or whatever . . .''

"SIKIM. The SIKIM-1000.''

"Whatever. I don't care what it's called, the whole idea is quite insane. Reggie will never approve! This is crazy.''

"So what, Maddy? This unit is crazy. We operate with a very broad charter, as you know. I don't need your permission to strike at Booker. You misled us to get us here to hit him in the first place. Now it turns out not at all tidy, not very British, and you want us to go home. As I said, I don't need your permission. I *do need* your cooperation. We'll just tell good old Farky after it's over. How will that be?''

"Oh, do! Oh, just let's do it!'' shouted Penelope.

"Shut up, you silly little twit! Don't you understand what this madman is suggesting?'' Madeline's pale skin was flushed, pink with exasperation.

"I think I understand perfectly, and I'll thank you not to call me names again unless you want that bleached blond hair of yours pulled out by its dark roots. He wants me to drive the double-decker bus while he and Steven, and I suppose you too, shoot at the men who tried to dishonor me at their leisure in that stinkin' alley. And I say bloody yes, let's shoot at them! Nobody can drive that bus like I can!''

Taken aback by Penelope's spirited attack on her as well as her enthusiasm, Madeline could only laugh and throw up her hands in surrender. "Well, I can only say this. If she's further involved in this, she'll have broken enough British laws to put her away until she rots. You'll probably have to take her with you when this is over."

"What do you mean, take her with us?"

"As I said. You shall have to take her with you, back to the States. Otherwise, we stop right now."

Penelope jumped to her feet and spun around the room, grabbing a bottle of champagne left in an ice bucket to chill. "To the Stick-it-100 or whatever it is! To buses! To Steven! To good sex and loving eyes! And to Penelope James, soon of the colonies!" Her pert buttocks nearly exposed, she raced around, handing out glasses and filling them, licking the spills off her fingers like popsicles, a charming display of emotion from a girl/woman clearly from another galaxy. "To us! To the stroke-it-100! To my wonderful Steven, who is going to marry me one day, like it or not!"

As they drank that improbable toast, Madeline said in a voice filled with both wonder and amusement, "I take it then, the mission is definitely on, Mr. Duggan?"

"So it would seem. How to do it, I'm not sure. But the mission is definitely on."

Penelope danced over and plunked herself in Steven Dye's lap. The meeting, for the moment, seemed to be completed.

Gresham Hotel
Folkstone, England

The Gresham Hotel advertised itself as a place "with home comfort and holiday pleasure." A family hotel with friendly personal service from resident proprietors. It was a blue-gray, spired and turreted throwback to the early 20th century. But on this day, it was the temporary home for a nest of spies and the SIKIM-1000, a 21st century supergun finally opened for viewing to the loosely formed spy community of Folkstone.

Michael Barns had called this early morning meeting at the insistence of Con Duggan. All five members of the United States team were there. "Farky" Farquarson and Madeline with six other dubious onlookers made up the British anti-terrorist unit. Penelope James, too, was there, hanging onto Steven Dye's arm, her eyes dancing with excitement.

She told everybody within earshot that she was going to "drive the bloom'n' bus and shoot the bloom'n'

111

Aussies' asses off.'' Which all came out as sort of a
one-word sentence punctuated by bouncing breasts and
enthusiasm. The British were appalled. So were the
Americans, except for Con Duggan and Steven Dye, who
seemed to not only enjoy Penelope's outbursts but welcome her active participation as well. Maddy cornered
Farquarson and tried to explain Penelope's admittance to
a circle so tight that few in either government knew of its
existence.

The Gresham Hotel lounge was not very spacious, but
there was plenty of room for the SIKIM-1000, backpack
and all. The agents crowded around the weapon, silenced
by its sleek but somehow massive bulk, its sighting system nearly as large as the weapon itself. Even Penelope
was quiet as Steven Dye explained what the SIKIM could
do and what limitations it had that he had yet to engineer
changes to offset. He explained the multiple barrels and
the multiple calibers the weapon could use in a normal
shooting mode. He explained the TAD round without
much detail except to say it could burn down Parliament
with two hits. Finally, he explained the backpack, how
the pack supplied the power for the TAD as well as the
EDR, or Energy Depletion Round, which he held up for
all to see. From the back, Penelope let out a gasp as she
saw the shape of the round, which always brought out
lascivious comments from the men when they first saw it.
After all, it did look like a multicolored dildo. A big one
at that.

''I'll surely need that, Steven Dye, if anything happens
to you. I felt you, you know!'' Steven Dye had no idea
what she meant, but from the look in her eye, he knew it
was trouble.

''I beg your pardon, Penelope?''

''That big colorful thing you have in your hand.''
Innocence never sounded more suspect.

''The EDR?''

''Yes. The EDR. The Enormous Dick Replacement! If
misfortune should strike you, Steven darling, I get the
EDR!''

The Gresham Hotel Lounge
3:00 A.M.

Michael Barns and Reggie Farquarson had been huddled
together away from Con Duggan and Steven Dye, who
were still accompanied by the other players in this night's
drama. Penelope James and Madeline were shooting a
game of snooker, and as far as Con could tell, getting
fairly drunk in the process. The business of secret intelligence seemed to have degenerated into an off-Broadway
or Kensington play about morality and its uses or abuses.
For his part, he was happy to see it this way. Steven Dye,
sipping Scotch, was just happy to watch two young
women in tiny skirts and tinier underwear lean over the
table to make shots neither of them could make, even if
they were serious about it, which they weren't. Peter Coy
Booker seemed a long way off. And as Con watched
Maddy clap her hands in embarrassment over a missed
shot, Maggie seemed far off as well. Con Duggan figured
if they received the go-ahead to shoot, he most likely
would get killed. He watched the sleek back of Maddy's
leg as she leaned far over the table. He felt very young
and very old at the same time.

Now Michael Barns was pressing his point with Farquarson. "Tell me, Reggie, what would be the conse-
quences if we go after Mr. Booker?" he asked.

"Do you mean as far as my government is concerned?"

"Yes, I mean exactly that."

"As you might imagine, Mr. Barns, if anything goes
wrong . . ."

"And any number of things might, and probably will,
go wrong."

"Oh, quite! Quite true! As I was saying, my government would officially frown, and without doubt, con-
demn the entire enterprise as misguided tomfoolery,

about which we, Her Majesty's Government, knew nothing at all.''

"I'm familiar with the see-no-evil abilities of governments to deny.''

"Are you? Do you have experience along that line?''

"Yes. I have experience along that line.''

Bon Tek Hamlet On The Cambodian Border
October 7, 1972

Michael Barns stood over the hulk of a man he had known intimately for almost eight years. Con Duggan was sitting cross-legged in the doorway of the hamlet chief's hootch, the only sounds in the firelit night the jungle scream of a big cat and the cacophany of night birds overhead. Only a faint, rust-colored band over the horizon spoke of the shattered day, shattered for Michael Barns when his observation helicopter was called in to pick up what he'd thought was Con Duggan. The man in the uniform looked like Con Duggan if you didn't look into his haunted, terrible eyes. Con's jaw clenched and unclenched in time to some unheard music from the past.

"How long has he been here?"

"A hunting slick on a free-kill flight spotted him on the other side of the border. About twenty miles. He was sittin' there, just like he is now."

"And? What other details do you have?"

"Not much, Major. Twenty or thirty NVA all around him in the bush. The chopper went into a hot L.Z. Burned out hootch, unidentified bodies inside, fifteen, maybe twenty more dead that had been trying to get at him. When the chopper went in, they had to pull him out of a log bunker. He kept trying to go back. Said some-fucking-thing about leaving his child. Sergeant Wolfe had to knock him cold and carry him to the chopper. Since then, he won't move. Just sits there, turned to stone, holding onto that fucking '03 like it was God or some go-to-hell

*goddamn thing! Corps is sending up a guy to get him. A
Colonel Fallon. You know him?''*

"Yeah. I know him.''

Folkstone, England
1992

"Well, then, old chap, if you have experience along the
thin line of government look-away, why in the bloody
hell do you want to do this? I know, we brought you here,
and I'll grant you that was on the shady side of the street,
but hell, man, we've accomplished all we must under
these rather ... rather exotic circumstances. I mean,
Penelope James! Gad, she might have been killed!''

"What you mean is, it would have been better if she
had.''

"You said it. I didn't.'' Reggie Farquarson had a tight,
very nasty smile on his face.

Bon Tek Hamlet
October 7, 1972

*Colonel Anton Fallon was a very impressive-looking
man. Close-cropped white hair. Piercing blue eyes.
Crisp, salty-looking fatigues bloused over boots spit-
shined daily by his newest "boy" orderly. A brightly
blued Colt Python rode high on his hip. He carried a
walking stick with an ivory-headed python at its top and
a fifty-caliber casing with a bullet at its tip. In spite of
over six years in country, he was still as pale-skinned as
he'd been in rainy Maine. He was, if you were inclined
that way, a "beautiful man.''*

"This is not good, Major Barns.''

"Sir?''

*"This will not wash. We had a big blowout scheduled
at headquarters. Big feed laid in and a couple of dozen
slits from Da Nang. Good slits, too!''*

"I'm not sure I follow you, Colonel Fallon." Formal. Very formal. But Michael followed him all too well.

"I talked a lot back in Saigon. I spoke just yesterday to the President."

"Ours, sir?"

"You know perfectly well who I mean, Barns."

"Of course, sir. Theirs."

"The South Vietnamese President and his staff had looked forward to honoring Sergeant Duggan. Unofficially, of course. One hundred kills! Thirty-eight of them poly officers! God, he was incredible! I had lunch with him a short time back. He took me with him, scouting the girl. Slim. Slim as a young boy, she was."

"Sir?"

"The NVA sniper. Did he get her?"

"Yes, sir. He did."

"Outstanding. He was a hell of a man!"

"Colonel Fallon, Sergeant Duggan is right here. He is not yet a 'was'!" Michael Barns struggled to keep himself under control, trying not to kill the faggot son-of-a-bitch with·his own walking stick.

"Well, Major. Yes, of course, and your point is well taken. I only meant, it doesn't look like he'll ever shoot again."

"He'll shoot, Colonel. If he wants to."

"Not for us, he won't. Not that he ever did, officially, did he? Too bad about the dinner. I'll be on my way, Major. Clean this up now. No loose ends. I'll send a medi-vac with clearance to Saigon and on to the States. You'll see to it?"

"Of course, sir. I'll pick up the trash. No loose ends." Lightning flashed in Michael's eyes.

"Good man!"

Ten days later, a fragmentation grenade attached to a bottle of champagne blew Colonel Anton Fallon's head off. No loose ends . . .

Con Duggan, motioned over to join the two team leaders, so alike in spite of their nationalities and upbringing, knew there was disagreement. The two men were sitting stiffly apart, staring into the Gresham's always-burning fireplace. He felt at home, somehow, in the cold dampness of England. Sometimes in Alaska, the mail planes didn't even fly in this soup. But he knew if it held on, he could still shoot in it.

"Farky here doesn't approve of our plan."

"Bloody hell, Mister Barns, but you've presented no plan!" Reggie looked properly officious and indignant too. Con Duggan broke into a hearty laugh, finally stopping to light a cigarette.

"Well, Mr. Duggan! Have you a plan?"

"Yes. Not a big, well-thought-out-plan. But a plan."

"Well. Speak up, man, or Her Majesty's Government is not interested!"

"Okay. I take Steven and the SIKIM and myself on the bus. Penelope drives."

"Ridiculous!"

"As I said, Penelope drives. Michael and Madeline handle the agents ashore in a combined operation with all on-site agents from our team. You, of course, have overall command, and I'm sure will refine my plan as you see fit."

"Me? In overall command? Well, I say. It's not a *bad* plan, Mr. Duggan. It needs a bit of refining, but overall it seems workable. There's Penelope, of course! Bad show, a mite of a civilian girl with too bloody much adrenaline . . ."

"Our problem."

"Yes, by God, Duggan. You'll have all responsibility for her, but overall . . ."

"We'll do it then?"

"Booker is here. Who knows when we'll have the chance again? Your plan is fine, Duggan, but it needs a bit of . . . a bit of . . ."

"British refinement?"

"Just so! British refinement. Now, you'd best go look at that bus. Might not be suitable for the 'Sikem.' The Sikem, right, Duggan?"

"Just so, Farky. Just so . . ."

• • •

To Steven Dye, the double door to the shed looked like it had not been opened in a quarter of a century. He was almost right. It had actually been forty years.

"Penelope, what are we doing here? And how do you intend to open that padlock?"

"I don't have a key, if that's what you mean."

"No key?"

"Not one. Shoot it off."

"Shoot it off?"

"The bloody lock. Shoot it off."

"Penelope, I don't shoot locks off of garages on foggy nights in the United Kingdom."

"I thought not. Your Mr. Duggan gave me this." With a Mona Lisa smile, if Mona Lisa had been sitting on a *very* pliant dildo, she handed him a fully loaded .45 auto mag. pistol.

"I don't shoot short guns, Penelope. You do it."

"Oh, goody. I like a man with big, long ideas." With that, she blew the lock and a third of the door off, holding the .45 until it stopped firing. Most guns do, when they are empty.

"Jesus fucking Christ, what are you doing?"

"I doubt that."

"What?"

"That Jesus could fuck Christ."

"I didn't mean . . ."

"I know, Steven. Now, help me push open the door."

"Why don't we just walk through the hole you blasted in the wall?"

"And I thought Yanks had no smarts. Steven! I'm impressed."

What was left of the garage door yielded to only a slight push. Steven turned on his flashlight and finally saw the double-decker bus he'd been led to believe would be perfect for the SIKIM-1000. What he saw was a very old green bus with a bright yellow stripe running the length of its still-polished sides. He also saw that it was up on blocks, without tires, and as far as he could tell, without any chance of actually running.

"It has no wheels?"

"Is that a question, Steven?"

"Hell no! It has no wheels."

"Ah, but it does have wheels. It has no tires, but it does have wheels."

Steven walked around the bus, trying to determine if it would ever run or carry his weapons system.

"Penelope, this is not a bus. This is a relic!"

"True on both counts. It's a relic that happens to be a bus."

"This is what you are charging us nine thousand pounds for? Where the hell is the bus company bus?"

"This is the bus company bus."

"No it's not. It won't run, and it has no open upper deck! Where am I going to mount the gun? Goddamn it, why did you do this?"

Penelope moved to his side and pulled him to her, her arms around his neck.

"I can drive it, Steven. All you have to do for the suckem is break out the glass on the upper deck. I'll help you. I lied to you, but only a bit. I *can* drive double deckers. I just never have."

Steven Dye looked into Penelope James's eyes while he was simultaneously pulling her body against his own. She looked at that instant like the answer to all his worst nightmares. Naturally, he let her lead him on.

"This won't work, Penelope."

"Yes it will. The engine runs."

"How do you know that?"

"Because English engines *always* run."

"How about the fucking tires?"

"They are right here in the shed."

"Can you change tires?"

Penelope thrust her hips against his. "*We* can change tires. You start, and I'll get the engine running."

"How? How will you do that?"

"My mum. She could build engines. During the war. Before she died, I got her Crosley running."

"Her what?"

"Her Crosley."

The bus, a 1939 Bristol K5G, was a 53-seater. It was waxed and polished, and the tires were properly inflated. It still had an old "Corona" advertisement on the upper level and "Westcliff on Sea" in gold lettering on the sides.

"I don't understand this, Penelope. This old bus is practically spotless. Winches to lift it for the tire change, clean lugs, spotless engine."

"Old Bob."

"Old Bob? What's an old Bob?"

"A chap that works on the buses. He once worked for Eastern Coach Works. They built this bus before the war. He worked there. He says he worked on this very bus. He must be at least 80. He loves this bus. It's a shame we shall have to break out the windows on the upper deck."

"Well, if this is the bus, that's exactly what we'll have to do. I can't mount the SIKIM on the fucking roof. This is crazy. Absolutely crazy."

"Yes, isn't it though. Old Bob is going to be brassed off, plenty brassed off, as me mum used to say."

Steven and Penelope, working in the dim light cast by two 150-watt bulbs hanging down from the dusty ceiling, had a surprisingly easy time of getting the tires on the bus. Old Bob had every tool imaginable. Each tire had ten lugs, all lightly oiled and easy to tighten. The wheels were carefully greased. Penelope hummed some child's song, scurrying around under and over the bus, grease collecting on her t-shirt, her cheeks, and nose. It all seemed like a school lark, a game, if you forgot for a moment what they intended to use the coach for. A mobile assault platform for the supergun. Judge, jury, and executioners on wheels. There were eighteen windows surrounding the upper deck. A two foot wide shelf of steel plate separated the lower and upper deck seating, with a steel roof overhead.

Penelope walked past Steven as he tightened the last lug on the last tire. Her face was dirty, her pert breasts bouncing as she scrambled onto the bus and up to the upper deck. "Down below, darling. Watch your sweet head." A hammer swinging in each hand, Penelope began to smash the glass from every other window, showering the shed floor and sending Steven scampering out of the way, and finally, all the way out of the shed for protection. Outside, he ran into Reggie Farquarson, Maddy, and Con Duggan.

"What in God's name is going on, young man?" Even in the dim light of the foggy courtyard, Steven could see the look of indignation on Farky's face.

"It's just Penelope, folks, smashing a bus window. Lots of bus windows. When it's quiet in there, we'll go in. Until then, trust me, it's a hell of a lot safer out here."

The four stood in the fog, while inside, glass continued to shatter and fall to the shed floor, to shatter again.

"Remember, Con, you agreed to take that young woman back to the States. I shall definitely hold you to that promise." Maddy gave Con Duggan a less-than-sympathetic smile.

Finally, the last window yielded to Penelope's free-swinging hammer, and she shouted the all-clear to Steven. He and the others entered the shed to find Penelope now wielding a large push broom, clearing a path for the bus to leave the shed. They watched with some fascination as she neatly piled the glass against the far wall. A small cut from flying glass was apparent at the corner of her mouth. Steven walked to her and touched the trickle of blood gently. It didn't look bad.

"You've cut yourself."

"That's all right. I kind of fancy the taste of blood. Sexy, don't you think?" Before he could reply, she pulled him to her and kissed him. He too could taste the blood.

"Like I said, Yank, I think blood is sexy." Penelope stepped around him and faced the team leaders.

"How do you like my lovely bus? We can certainly shoot them all from this, don't you think?" Quickly while the others gaped at her, she ran back to the bus, hopped in, and started the engine. It burst to life immediately, running very smoothly in spite of its old age. Old Bob had done some remarkable things to the old Eastern Coach Works bus. Even without most of its upper deck glass, it looked fully capable of carrying fifty-three passengers anywhere they might need to go. Already, though, Steven Dye was looking at it for what it would be tonight. A gun platform.

Aboard The Stingray
Folkstone Harbor
5:45 A.M.

The room was dark, lit only by candles placed near the bed. A woman lay face down on the bed, her legs spread-eagled, her ankles tied loosely to the bedpost, as were her hands. Her bonds were not too tight. She could free herself if she wanted to. Crouched between her wide open thighs, another woman smoothed oil across the woman's quivering buttocks, occasionally slipping her fingers deep between her legs. Pulling against her bonds, the "captive" would then twist and arch her hips against the magic fingers of the faceless woman behind her. There were four other women in the room, hovering above the writhing form on the bed, eight soft hands and four hot mouths coming at her from every angle. It was a very big bed. Soon all five woman were locked together. The room reeked of sex and oil and candle wax. Finally, the silent woman tied to the bed screamed out in the throes of sexual release before quieting down to a whimpering, hip-rolling state of satiation. The other women pulled away, closing the cabin door behind them, and she was left alone.

But only for a moment. The door opened and a man entered. He sat in a chair, then moved to the bed, untying the woman. She rolled over, and he bent forward and kissed first one erect nipple and then the other. She looked up at the man, her eyes worshipful, her arm across his lap. Quickly, he wrapped her arm with a piece of surgical rubber, and then he reached for a small vial, inserting the stainless steel hypodermic needle, drawing the liquid up into the needle. In the dim light, he found her arm, the vein prominent and ready. She gasped as the needle slid into her, involuntarily opening her thighs, as the drug she needed rushed to her brain and throughout her body, a kind of non-sexual climax. She gave the man a grateful smile, kissed his hand, and tried to pull it down to her arched and open thighs. The man pulled free and sat down in the chair. Eyes bright in the candlelight, her veins full, her heart pulsing, coursing, and delivering the powerful drug to every nerve ending, the woman gave the man a disappointed pout.

"I want you to fuck me. I need to be fucked."

"Not now, Madeline. Now I want you to tell me why it was necessary for you to kill Dorsey Talbot." Booker was very angry.

Madeline had first met Booker two years before in the Caribbean. The Stingray *had dropped anchor, and she had watched the small fleet of Zodiacs head to shore through the bright sun, paying it no more attention than all the other boats of all sizes that bobbed at anchor in the paradise harbor she had chosen for her first vacation in five years. Only one other employee had risen so fast in the agency, and it had taken him only one year less service. At twenty-seven, she was Farquarson's chosen one, a rising star.*

She stretched out and rolled over, digging her fingers into the white sand, pressing her bikinied body against the heat, reveling in the pure sensation of youth and freedom from care or worry.

She had felt him more than seen him. She knew she was

being looked at in the way women don't approve of. She'd fix him, whoever he was. She kept her face turned away and slowly, deliberately, opened her leg a bit. Occasionally, she would flex her muscles, tightening and releasing her buttocks. She could feel his eyes, but she didn't turn around. Soon her game backfired as her thighs moistened to the point of near climax. Embarrassed but excited, she sat up to face his voyeuristic presence. But she was alone. A hundred yards away, a powerfully built man dressed in white pants and a black shirt sat in a beach chair. Too far away. But if not him, who? Her bikini bottom clung to her, wetly outlined as she stood up to leave. Down the beach, the man raised his fingers to his lips and blew her a kiss.

Later that evening, dressed in a black strapless dress she'd bought at auction (because it had once been worn by the famous James Bond girl, Pussy Galore, in a movie) she'd had a bit of luck at the gaming tables. It had been a gay night, too much champagne, her luck too good, handsome men in abundance to fuss about her bare English skin, so pale even here in the sunny Caribbean. She felt busty and leggy and very interesting indeed.

She was winning at blackjack when the man from the beach chair sat down directly opposite her, dressed now in an expensive tuxedo, accompanied by three of the most exotic women she had ever seen. Oriental, but not alike. As if he'd picked them all from separate Asian countries. They wore very expensive gowns, all sequinned and beaded and pearled. But what startled her the most was the way they looked at her. She tried to pay attention to her cards but was drawn back time and time again to the three women until she recognized the look in their eyes. It was, she was sure, naked lust, potent and obvious. She felt her flesh heat as a flush of color swept upward from her feet to her forehead. She had been a lesbian for as long as she could remember, though she was probably more truly bisexual. But these women knew. And she knew the cruelly handsome man with the hard body and harder eyes knew it as well.

From that moment, Peter Coy Booker's seduction of Madeline had been ridiculously easy. Far from the confining restriction of the British Intelligence Service, heady with the tropic islands and champagne and money gambled as if there were no end to it, she had joined the exotic quartet at their table for the evening. It had seemed to her quite natural, though it was anything but that.

They had seemed to flow together, the three darkly seductive women and the pale blond English woman trailing along behind the man with the hard eyes. They did not touch her, at least in a sexual way. But they were beautiful and exciting, and Booker, as he asked her to call him, was elegantly, if a bit coldly, charming. After two hours of gambling, during which, to her astonishment, she discovered she'd won over twenty thousand pounds, they boarded a sleek speedboat and motored across the harbor to the pale brilliance of the moonlit Stingray.

It was reckless and exciting and liberating, and she had sex with each woman individually and finally all together, a blur of breasts and mouths and thighs and sex toys she had only fantasized about. Finally, out of her mind with need, she'd taken Booker as well, with two women under her and one draped over his back. They had drugs, and she asked questions and had more sex, and finally, she'd passed out. When she woke up, she was a drug-addicted dyke with a need for Peter Coy Booker and what he had to give her. He had tapes of her doing and having done to her. Things she loved but would never admit. But it wasn't really blackmail. She liked it, needed it, and would sell her soul or anything else to get it. There has been much said about drugs and sex used to co-opt male spies. It works just as well on female spies.

"I killed Dorsey because I had no choice. What was I to do, let him kill that girl, and Con Duggan's young friend as well? How much credibility would I have after that? Besides, I quite enjoyed it. The man could never keep his hands off me."

"You like hands on you. A lot of them, and I've never known you to be choosey."

"Oh, but I am. You have the magic formula, but he didn't. Anyway, he's dead. And so will you be if you don't pull anchor and sail out of Folkstone Harbor by nightfall."

"And who is going to kill me? I've done nothing."

"Con Duggan. The agency actually brought him here for just that purpose. I've not told you that because I didn't know exactly myself. But he will certainly try to kill you."

"When?"

"Tonight."

"How?"

Here, for her own reasons, Madeline lied. "I'm not sure. You know him better than I do."

"I'll not give him the bugger of a chance. I intend to remain on the *Stingray* until we sail. Probably the day after tomorrow. Ten of my men can take care of him ashore, don't you think?"

"Ten should do nicely, yes. Send them in here first, would you? I need to be fucked, and you won't fuck me."

"You know this is a do-it-yourself boat, Madeline. Why don't you just fuck yourself?"

"I will. Would you like to watch?"

"Some other time, luv. You'd better get back to shore. Your friends will have need of your services." He tossed her clothes at her and left the cabin. Tomorrow night, he would have to kill her.

Shortly before dawn, Con Duggan and Steven Dye, with the frenetic assistance of Penelope James, had finished preparing the bus for its mission. Seats had been removed from the top deck leaving only the seat backs at the open windows. The SIKIM could be shifted to any side, front or rear. The battery pack had been attached to the floor on a seat rail so it could slide the length of the bus. Sheet metal had been installed behind the driver's seat, although they could figure no way to protect her from the side. The bus really offered very little protection from anything, but Con had insisted on trying every possible idea to make it less vulnerable. The truth was, and it was Penelope who voiced it, the bus would look like green Swiss cheese if it was shot at.

"It's not a bloody tank, don't you know?" she'd said cheerfully. They left two agents with the bus and headed out of the shed for breakfast and some sleep. They planned to meet at the Gresham at 4:00 P.M. It would most likely be a long night.

"So, it's ready, is it?" Con was surprised to see Madeline emerge from the small car. She'd said she was going back to her hotel to sleep. That had been three hours ago. She was still wearing the same clothes. She seemed very nervous, her eyes unnaturally bright. Her voice was pitched a bit higher than usual.

"It's as ready as it will get, Maddy. Penelope says it's no tank, and she's right. You're going to have to contain or kill Booker's people ashore tonight, or this might not work out too well."

"You're going with me, at least for a while?"

"Well, sure, if you think you need me. How many people are we talking about?"

"Don't know, really. Ten or more, I should think. I just thought you might like to see me operate."

"Yeah, I'd like that."

"Good. See you at the Gresham then." She came to his side, as usual, to kiss his neck. He looked straight into her lovely, drugged-out eyes. He'd seen eyes like that before—every time he'd been around Booker.

"I'm dragging my lovely Steven off to my flat, Mr. Duggan. I'll see he gets to bed." Penelope laughed uproariously at that, pulling a not unhappy young man down the street after her.

"Four o'clock! Don't be late."

He got no answer and found himself alone in the early morning dampness of Mission Day in Folkstone.

• • •

Penelope was right. Her landlord did keep her flat warm. It was located on the hill above Folkstone. Steven could look out her window, the only window in the flat, and see both the Gresham and Langhorne Gardens Hotels. Beyond, as the day broke gray and foggy, he could not see the *Stingray* through the mist. But the SIKIM could. The SIKIM could do a lot of strange and wonderful things.

"Kiss me a little, Steven. Then I must take a shower. This may be a tiny flat and all, but I've got my own loo!" She kissed him. Very softly on the lips, her hands flat against his chest, her body just brushing his. She smelled of motor oil and grease and dirt and the musky smell that seemed to be all her own. She vanished behind a bright pink door, one of four wildly different colors that blanketed the walls. It was as if she'd painted the flat with whatever color she could find without regard to how it might blend. Soon he heard the water raggedly splashing against the tiny circular shower curtain he'd seen through the door.

He walked around the flat, a series of small rooms separated by paper-thin walls. None of the rooms was larger than an average-to-small American bedroom, and the kitchen was only about six or eight feet square. A tiny stove, small refer, a table, and two chairs. A mish-mash of dishes of all sizes and colors rested in a bright blue dish drainer near the sink.

The living room and bedroom were really one large room with a gaudy screen the only wall separating the living and sleeping areas. He glanced into the bedroom. Two beds, only inches apart, one made, one unmade. He tried to imagine what Penelope had described, she in bed while her cousin had sex with her boyfriend in the next bed. It was near impossible for him to picture it. If they were having sex in one bed, so would anybody in the other bed.

The walls were crammed with snapshots, some

framed, others just tacked to the walls or propped on the
flat's one bookshelf.

Steven Dye was not a student of family relations. He
had manufactured his own family, a sort of trip to Oz to
get heart and courage and brains, as applied to his mother
and father. Penelope had her life spread around the tiny
flat: mother, father, cousins, dogs, cats, picnics, and
Christmas. She hardly seemed the family type, and yet
she had photographic evidence he had only imagined or
dreamed about. What, he wondered, was it like to grow
up among so many branches of one's own lifeblood?
Relatives you could admit to, good or bad. Familiar faces,
faces from your past that would and did age as you aged.
He knew he had four half-brothers, but he also knew he
had never been acknowledged as such. He was the
product of lust, not family. His mother fucked his father
or vice versa, and here he was in England, plotting death
and destruction and sexual adventure in a flat full of
memories belonging to someone else.

Many of the pictures were in black and white. Strong-
faced young men standing in uniform next to fighter
planes, all white scarves and slovenly uniforms and
devil-may-care smiles about to face the Hun. Trim, anxious women, with good legs and sensible shoes and the
look of the warily hopeful. He *will* come back to me.
Birthdays, funerals, shopping, fires, and dances and wild
celebrations. There were pets, too. Dogs, cats, small
ponies with smaller children on their flanks. A wall of
portraiture from the nineteen forties.

The black-and-white photos gave way to the sepia and
bad color of the sixties, Polaroids, older people, whiter
hair. Children now with grandchildren, puppies with old
dogs, small houses grown larger with time and money
and prosperity. No sign of social change, no sign of
radical thought, only families moving up.

Scenes from disco dances and drunken balls and
women wearing mini-skirts from Carnaby Street. British
bands, later to be famous, famous bands, later to be
British. Penelope's walls were a treasure history in Ko-

dak and Polaroid and finally, Fuji film, shot as fast as the camera could work. There was a whole wall of the flat devoted to smiling, handsome young men, well dressed, well fed, prosperity shining from their smiles and off their leather coats. He studied the pictures, the sound of the shower fading, and his early thoughts of what Penelope looked like in the shower fading with it. He couldn't find Penelope in *any* of the photographs. He lit a cigarette, snuffed it out, lit another. She was nowhere to be found. He went back to the black-and-white photos, looking for . . . for what? Parents? Sisters? Brothers? The toilet flushed, flushed again. Where on this wall of history and family was Penelope James?

Penelope emerged from the bathroom, a white towel wrapped turbanlike around her head, covering her long black hair. She wore a baggy terrycloth robe, tattered and thin and a bad shade of brown. He could see her feet and the flash of an ankle bracelet. Her heels were bright red and four inches high.

"I always wear heels, Steven, because I'm only five feet three without 'em. I have a strange body. Half of me goes from my head to my waist. The other half goes from my waist to my feet. Heels make me taller and my legs seem longer. Trust me, Yank, heels are best."

"You look wonderful, Penelope."

"Yes, I do, don't I? I put on fresh lipstick, eye shadow, and a quart or two of Joy perfume, mostly between my legs, right on top of my butterfly."

"Your butterfly?"

"Yes. I have a butterfly tattooed between my legs. Tell me, Steven, are you left thighed or right thighed?"

"I'm sorry?"

"What I mean is, do you like one thigh better than the other?"

"I don't think I have a preference."

"I just wondered. My butterfly thigh, my right thigh, is more sensitive. So when you eat my pussy, pay attention to the butterfly!"

Penelope sat down on the tattered divan before Steven

could comment on her butterfly. There was a small end table cluttered with nail polish next to the divan. She selected one and pulled the robe above one knee, removing a high-heeled shoe in the same motion. She rested a long slim foot on the cushion and opened the nail polish.

"I'm going to paint my toenails, Steven. Have you ever watched a woman paint her toenails?"

"No." His voice creaked, another man's voice from another place and time.

Penelope stretched her leg out, the robe pulling up and over her thighs. A dark triangle appeared between her legs, and he could look at nothing else. As she brushed and stroked the Chinese red across her toenails, the robe pulled loose, her leg alabaster white, sleek and firm and more.

"Toes should be red, don't you think? I went through stages, bloody stupid, but I did. Black! Can you imagine? Blue! Yellow nails! Looked like I had the bloomin' plague! Finally, red, this red, seemed best. What do you think, Steven Yank?" She extended her leg, resting her foot on his lap, her eyes smoldering black coals, ancient eyes, child eyes, woman's eyes.

"I want to see the butterfly."

"And so you shall, Steven. But at my pace."

"I hate to admit this, Penelope, but *I* have no pace. Yours will do just fine."

"Good. Now watch me. It will excite you, I hope. Well, no, I don't hope. I *know* it will excite you. Now, Steven, I have done a toe. Will you do the rest? Paint them, Steven. Paint them for us."

Penelope raised her foot from his lap to his chest, planting it and leaning back.

"Paint them, Steven. Look for the butterfly, talk to me, and paint my toes. Red. Very red. When they are dry, I'm going to wrap them around your head, so you can see my butter . . . fly."

Steven Dye was not a sophisticated young man. He acted the part, but Penelope James had blown his cover. He took her foot in his hand, tracing the arch with his fingers. She twisted her foot, pulling the tattered, unsexy terrycloth robe even higher. Now he could see very clearly the dark vee of her pussy, and, he thought, the butterfly.

"It's on your left thigh?"

"Asking or tellin'?"

"Telling. It's on your left thigh."

She pulled her sleek legs together, extending both feet, burrowing into his lap. Flexing, touching his hard-on.

"Paint, Steven. We'll see if you're right later."

Her heels were resting on each side of his crotch as he painted her toes, and at each brush stroke, she wiggled her feet. Somehow, the top of her robe had pulled to her waist. There was now only a puddle of robe at her waist extending to her hips. She had thrown her head back on the couch pillow, and she was kneading her breasts, pulling on her nipples, calling his name. One leg was flung wide, then the other.

"Put the heels back on my feet, Steven Dye!"

"But I'm not finished."

"Put them on. I want to *mark* you!"

He fumbled with the red heels, Penelope arching her feet, helping him. Somehow he got them on her. And then she was up and pulling him down to her. As he moved downward on her, trying to match her ferocity with his own, he could not for the life of him remember which thigh had the butterfly.

"You lied to me. There *is* no butterfly." Steven croaked as he drew close to her.

She pulled his face into her, her thighs trembling, enveloping him. "Yes! Yes! There! I lied to you! Suck me, Steven, swallow me whole!"

But there *was* a butterfly, a very tiny tattoo. Its body was between her breasts. One wing on one breast, one wing on the other. It was a whole insect if you pushed her breasts together. And later it flew like a butterfly with Steven thrusting at her, her hands making a kind of hot cushion, her eyes hotter, looking up at him, her tongue flicking at him, controlling him while setting him, like the butterflies, free.

They had retreated behind the screen, and therefore, technically, into the bedroom. Penelope had pushed the two small beds together. Even combined, the two beds made a very small double bed. It hardly mattered, because Steven and Penelope were either in, on, or pressed together. A bed a quarter of the size of the two would have been large enough. Passion doesn't need a lot of space.

"Tell me about the pictures." Steven said after they'd recovered.

Penelope lay curled over him, her thigh against his temporarily sated penis, her breast and one butterfly wing was crushed against his thin but muscular chest. "What about them, hon?" Her back was hot to the touch, her thighs damp, her whole body giving out a kind of steamy heat.

"Who are they all? I'm not from a large family, an only child, so I'm interested in families like yours."

"An only child? Good thing, too. Don't know what I'd do if there were two of you." She gave his flaccid penis a little pat, a kind of job-well-done pat. He was surprised to find himself rising under her slim fingers. She quit patting him, running her nails down his length, cupping him. Her tongue flicked at his nipple, and she slid up to his neck, kissing him.

"Penelope! Jesus, I'm not a machine."

"I am, Steven, and you're goin' to love it."

"Stop for a minute. Tell me about the pictures." He pulled back, but not very far.

"All right then." She sat up, crossing her legs, brushing her long dark hair back across her slim neck. She had the palest skin he'd ever seen, made more so by the contrast with her hair. He was very taken with her, though she confounded him most of the time. Butterflies in three pieces. Total sexual abandon. Humor. And something else. Something dark and unknown. She was tough in ways more male than most males. On balance, she scared the shit out of him.

"None of the pictures are my family. In point of fact, Yank, none of the pictures in this flat are of anybody I know. I buy them at flea markets, at fairs, wherever I can find them. I had pictures of my mum, and once, I think, of my aunt. You remember, the vicar's wife?"

"Oh, yeah. No fucking with the lights on." He had a vision of fumblings in the dark, skirts and clerical collars flying like bats.

"Right. That's her." Penelope moved then, straddling him, her back to him, her hand bringing him back to hard life. She moved almost imperceptibly, and they were joined again. She leaned back, her knees supporting her, her back against his chest, her damp hair sweet against his mouth. Bent that way, she could still move her pelvis, and she did. Apparently, when Penelope didn't want to talk, she fucked . . . "Grab my hair, Steven Dye. Grab my hair and pull." She whimpered then, and her hips began to fly.

"When I was a very little girl, my mum began to have what I'll call a number of gentlemen callers. Quite a large number, if I recall. And I do." They were at the tiny kitchen table drinking tea, a couple taking a break from examining each other's bodies to the even more intimate examination of each other's psyches. "She had a problem, mum did. She thought she couldn't do anything proper, but she was a very sexy little Eastender, and the Westenders came by to pay their respects. Mum was a prostitute."

"You don't have to tell me any of this, Penelope. It's none of my business."

"No, it's not. But one day I will bear your children, and I'll not have you worrying about ancestry and lineage. Mine is not good. There. Now you'll not have to worry your red little head. She, my mum, was an immoral tramp. And so am I, else why would I have tattooed tits and a yen to swallow you whole?"

"Easy. I'm irresistible." He gave her a warm smile, a smile from a lover, a smile from a friend. "Now, tell me the whole story. Not just the parts you use to shock me. Your mother was a hooker. So what? Mine was a drunk and died from it. But she was terrific. A *nice* woman in spite of it all."

She gave him a very serious look and sipped at her tea before going on. "My mother was more than my mum. She was only fourteen when I was born. I never met my father. She wasn't entirely sure who it was, actually. A seaman, I think. So here she was, herself and me in her arms to feed. I know it's a bloody awful old story, but she sold herself because she had no one and no way to feed me. When I was thirteen, we began to share the load, you might say. We worked together in Paris and Amsterdam. A mother-daughter team. Ten years ago, my mother and I were paid ten thousand dollars for my virginity, lost in a hot threesome. The madam resold my virginity for over two years. About one hundred times, until my mum just walked away one day and never came back. I stayed in Paris for a while with a painter. A gypsy type, ya know. Always steal'n' and drink'n' and after my bum. His mother did the butterfly tattoo. One night, he came home drunk with two friends. I wasn't much, of course, whorin' like I was. But they held me down and raped me. Even whores can be raped. They went off later, and my gypsy fell asleep. I stuck a butcher knife in his neck and left it there. Kicked around for a while, workin' a mortuary once, makin' up the corpses and washing the hearse. I went through a few more bad men and ran a tobacco shop and sold ice creams from a truck at Brighton. Then you found me, and now you're stuck with me. So Steven, what do you say to that?"

Steven could think of nothing at all to say.

"Are you shocked, Steven?"

"Yeah. A little bit."

"Well, you'll get over it. More tea?" She got up and poured him more tea, her sleek body exposed as the robe fell open.

"No more tea." He pulled her to him and fucked her right there on the table, tea cups bouncing and crashing against the floor as her legs went high over his shoulders. He'd never been more excited in his life.

Con sat in the darkened suite of the Langhorne Gardens staring out across the harbor, trying to penetrate the thick fog. A faint glow of red and orange brightened the fog where he thought the *Stingray* was anchored. But he couldn't be sure. He wanted to see the boat to reassure himself that he had a target, that Booker had not simply weighed anchor and gone back to Australia, richer than ever and still alive. He wondered about Steven Dye and his visit to and with Penelope James. They made quite a pair. Volatile. Oversexed. Young. And in Steven's case, far out of his natural element.

What had he seen in Madeline's eyes? Drugs? Excitement? Both? What was wrong here? Her eyes. What did they tell him? What, except to watch his back. Nothing new . . .

Camp 8A, CIA Branch Center, Camp San Onefre, Camp Pendleton, California October, 1973

Most of all, he didn't like her eyes. Con Duggan had been looking at her eyes for almost six months. He liked her high breasts. He liked her mouth. He liked her skirts, a bit shorter than most naval officers would wear. Her legs were short, too, and a little too full at the ankle. Still, not bad for a lieutenant commander. His shrink had better legs than most naval officers, and he was grateful for that small favor. But he didn't like her eyes. Her eyes looked out, but you could not look in. Dark blue. Not pretty eyes. Just blue.

"Do you still see the little girl, Sergeant? You haven't mentioned her in over two weeks." She never called him anything but sergeant. A way to keep things official, she

said. *One bitch officer to one bastard Marine in the agency's employ, as well as it's doghouse.*

"Yeah, I still see her. I'll always see her."

"Well, perhaps not always."

"Yes, always."

"We hope not, but we'll work on it, won't we?"

"If you say so."

"Your Michael Barns is here to see you."

"He's here a lot, but he's not *my* Michael Barns."

"Yes. He cares about you, Sergeant Duggan. He has left foreign duty to take up duties here for a while. We, I mean I, want you to be fully capable of returning to duty. Until you are, you will stay here. Michael Barns will stay here too."

"I'm not going back. I'm not shooting. Not ever again."

"We—I—am not trying to make you well just so you can go back in country and . . . and . . ."

"Shoot people. I shoot people. Women. Kids. Anything you got. Confirmed kills. All of them. I'm a hell of a guy, don't you think? Tell me, Doc, don't you think I'm a hell of a guy?" He jumped to his feet, reaching her chair before she could move. He pulled her up and off her feet, holding her by her uniform collar, her body against his, her eyes—so blue—only inches from his.

"Are you scared, Doctor Navy? No. I didn't think so. But I'm not going to fuck you—or let you fuck me. I'm not going to cooperate. I'm not going to resist, either. I'm going to take what I know and walk away, and sooner or later, you're going to give up on me. I'm not shooting. Do you understand that? Marilyn Monroe and Rita Hayworth could suck my dick and my ass simultaneously, and I wouldn't shoot. Give it up, Navy! Give it up." He dropped her back into her chair, sat down, and lit a cigarette.

"Well, Sergeant, you're beginning to show some life! Good! Very good. We'll talk again tomorrow."

Con never saw her again. But he remembered her empty eyes. It takes a shooter to know a shooter.

• • •

Peter Coy Booker, like all other players in the drama scattered around Folkstone that foggy night, was also awake. Had he been able to, he would have fixed his gaze on the Langhorne Gardens. He too was blocked by the fog. If it suddenly lifted, the two men would be revealed to each other. But no matter. Both men had plans for each other, fog or no fog.

Booker was mounting machine-guns throughout the *Stingray*. He wasn't worried about Con Duggan shooting him. There were *rules* for the civilized spy agencies, and one longstanding rule was nobody shot him unless they *caught* him doing something. Still, the British were very odd at times. An ambitious agent eager to please an equally ambitious government minister might decide to chase down the *Stingray* at sea. Bad idea, that one! But if it came to a naval battle with a flimsy British cutter, he intended to win. Rules. Yes, the British and the Americans, *particularly* the Americans, still played by the rules. Booker could, and intended, to kill Con Duggan. Rules were to be broken, and Booker was very good at breaking them. Pick up his toys. Kill Madeline. Kill Con Duggan and his young friend. Sail off, richer than ever, and satisfied as well. He would miss Madeline. But the world, his world, was full of Madelines.

"I'd like you to connect me to a phone number please."

"Of course, Mr. Duggan," said the desk clerk. Only downstairs from Con's suite, but the phone sounded like it was far away.

"The number, sir?"

"01-730-3488."

"Of course, sir. Will you hold?"

"Yes. I'll hold."

Con lit a cigarette and waited.

"Sir."

"Yes."

"Mr. Duggan, the number you gave me is the London Tourist Bureau."

"Did they answer?"

"Yes, sir."

"Fine. Ask for Moira Anderson, please."

"Yes, sir."

Con waited, his fingers drumming a jazz beat on the phone stand.

"Sir?"

"Yes."

"We have your Ms. Anderson."

"Thank you. Moira?"

"Mr. Duggan?"

"Who else? Connect me to 21A, will you?" He immediately felt bad about his abrupt answer, but not *real* bad.

"Yes, Mr. Duggan."

Con waited again and then heard the whine of machinery. Computers.

"This is 21A." The voice was young, crisp, efficient.

"Duggan here. We got any way to track individuals on that bird of ours?"

"Sure. What do you need?" Con was impressed. And he felt the power of who he was. It felt very good.

"Something nice. For a lady."

" 'Kay. We'll get back to you in a minute."

"I'll need them in four hours."

"Can do."

"How will I get them?"

"We deliver, Mr. Duggan." A smile in the voice now.

"Thanks, 21A."

"No problem, sir."

The line went dead. But Aircraft 21A, thirty-one miles outside London, never slept or rested. In twenty minutes, Con Duggan had what he needed loaded into a van and roaring down an English freeway toward Folkstone. The van carried a flower for Maddy. The flower had ears. . . .

Michael Barns popped another little black-and-red pill into his mouth, assuring himself of twenty-four hours of activity without thc need for sleep. The technicians aboard 21A had prepared as well as possible for the next night's events. The monitors blinked, the tapes ran on, and he could see at a glance the status of the mission. The C-130 wasn't just an airplane. It was a flying brain. At daybreak, it would take off and remain airborne until Booker was either dead or captured. Along one wall, a series of numbered lights overlaid on a map of Folkstone identified the British and American agents on ground as well as the last known positions of Booker's men.

An incredible amount of technology was stored and jammed into every available space on Aircraft 21A. Wherever the team was, 21A would be, whether 21A designated the black-painted hangar at Nellis Air Force Base or a car or bus or plane. 21A was the catchall number for the U.S. anti-terrorist team handled by Michael Barns. Fog locked England into a hundred-foot ceiling, but the unit's aircraft could fly in zero ceiling if required.

Michael Barns had spent thousands of hours in the field, many of them alone, or in support of Con Duggan, as was the case in Southeast Asia. At times, that support had consisted of no more than a Bowie knife chopping a trail through the jungle, putting the shooter in the right spot at the right time. Now Michael Barns was worried about his shooter. His friend. All the luxury provided by the 21A budget, its whistles and bells and money, would mean little if Con Duggan had not shaken his ghosts.

The Gresham Hotel
"Strike Force Booker" Headquarters
4:00 P.M.

Steven Dyc had not yet seen how many agents were involved in the multinational effort to kill Peter Coy Booker. Now in the sealed-off dining room of the Gresham, he counted twenty-three men and two women. He didn't know many of them, and he didn't expect to be introduced. Most were "bearers" whose job was to pinpoint and track Booker's people, wherever they were. Some were "clean-up" personnel, men whose job would be to tidy up after the shooters from the U.S. left town. Clearly, it was a new age in dealing with international thugs and terrorists. The kid gloves were off. In the future, the mailed-fist approach would rule both sides' activities. There would be shootouts all over the world from this night forward.

Con Duggan, Michael Barns, and Steven Dye, along with their enthusiastic new recruit, Penelope James, were sitting in a small cluster to the rear of the hall. The

SIKIM-1000, boxed and ready to take for a bus ride, served as Penelope's perch and viewpoint. She would alternately sit, stand, or dance on the box, depending on her mood. Con looked at her like a wayward daughter, Michael with trepidation, and Steven Dye with moony-eyed lust and other love emotions run amok. For her part, Penelope intended to shoot all the bad guys "seriously dead," as she put it. The men wore rough clothes, jeans and sweats for the most part. Penelope was wearing a beaded blouse under an oxford sweatshirt, a mini-skirt, and heels.

"Penelope," Steven whispered in between her alternate sitting positions on the SIKIM-1000 box, "don't you have any flat shoes? Tennies? Something like that?"

"No, Steven Yank, I don't. I have no pants of any kind, either. But you needn't worry. I do everything in high heels, as if you didn't know." She leaned forward and kissed his ear, her tongue washing it out like a cleaner in a wash basin.

"But how are you going to drive the bus in high heels?"

"I always drive in high heels! There was a bloke once in Amsterdam, when my mum and I were still together—working, I mean. He was a silly fat little man, and he didn't want normal sex, although I don't bloody know what normal sex is in any case. This little man had a shoebox, a rather big shoebox. He would open it up and take out this big board. He'd nailed a brake pedal, a clutch pedal, and an accelerator pedal to this board. Anyway, he'd have us take turns 'driving' him. He'd lay down, a little old, fat, silly man, and he'd hold the board across his chest. He insisted we wear hose and very high heels, and that's all. We would work the pedals with our feet, and he would look up at us, right up between our legs, and he'd go 'zoom-zoom,' like a car, and we would operate the pedals. Finally, he would come on himself, going 'zoom-zoom' the whole time while we shifted from pedal to pedal. Then he would clean up, give us each one hundred dollars, tip his conductors hat to us both, and leave. Believe me, Steven, I can definitely drive anything, heels on or heels off!''

To Penelope, that kinky little explanation settled the matter. She kissed his other ear, gave him a little crotch pat, and walked across the big room to the wet bar, hips rolling, a kind of tribute to his good taste. Every male eye followed those hips. If hips could be said to have a personality of their own, hers did. He was proud she cared for him. But she still scared him to death.

The lovely British spy finally opened the meeting.

"Gentlemen . . . and lady, may I have your attention, please.'' Madeline stood at the head of the room, a fold-up blackboard and a photographically blown-up street map of Folkstone behind her. She was wearing a one-piece, skintight, black body suit with a heavy black sweater that extended to her hips. A Browning semiauto pistol and extra clips fit snugly to her waist on a wide black belt. She wore black rubber-soled boots. She didn't look sexy. She looked very dangerous.

"The circled numbers on the map,'' here she used a pointer to tap each one, "are the Martello Towers. They were built to repel an invasion by the French, which didn't come until the Chunnel was built, which makes invasion by the French a reality.'' The British agents laughed at this, but it was pretty much an inside joke. Penelope frowned. She didn't like the French and she told Steven Dye she hoped "the bloody Chunnel sinks, preferably while full of Frenchmen.'' He had not pursued the matter.

"There are eight of them we're concerned with. They are all, quite naturally considering their intended use, along the shoreline.'' Again she pointed out the towers. A slide projector clicked on, focused on the white back wall of the hall. The towers looked like what they were, piles of formidable rocklike parts of a medieval toy set. Windows were cut in the top, and ramparts covered them as well. They seemed to offer very effective possibilities to a hit team. Booker's hit team, as it turned out.

"The number three tower, here, above East Cliff

Sands, looks down on Harbor Station, the harbor itself, and East Railway Station. Tower number four, here, looks down the throat of Leas Cliff, Leas Cliff Hall, the Langhorne Gardens Hotel, and, coincidentally, a good shot from there to this very room. We are sure of two teams of Booker's men, although surely not Booker himself, in those two towers. Tower number five covers Sandgate Castle, though we don't believe that is why they are there. If the *Stingray* pulls out, that position could cover them quite well. Three separate locations, nine men, we believe. They've been in there for quite some time. We're not sure how long or what weapons they may have. We do believe that those teams did not come here on the *Stingray*. If that is correct, they may still be part of an active shoot against the dignitaries this Friday. We shall have to deal with them in any event. We believe they are not regular members of Booker's entourage. We believe they are Palestinian mercenaries. We shall have to kill them, of course. They will not surrender. Con Duggan and I shall lead the attack on the Martello Towers, commencing at midnight.''

Con Duggan glanced at Michael Barns, who looked back, said nothing, but raised his hands, palms up, and shrugged. The slide show switched to exterior and interior shots of Leas Cliff Hall, the site of the model exhibition. ''We intend to blanket the hall prior to tonight's last public showing. When Booker or his agents return after closing, we shall intercept them and arrest them quietly, if possible. My superior, Mr. Farquarson, has chosen to conduct that operation himself, with twelve agents.''

''What about me and Steven Yank?'' Penelope, being Penelope, could not shut up. Patience was, for her, an undiscovered virtue.

''Steven . . . Steven Dye and Miss James, as his driver, will move the bus to whatever position is required during the early evening operations. The final operation, mounted against the *Stingray* itself, will be handled from the bus as well. This part of the operation is to be the exclusive domain of the American team, against my objections. I shall talk to Con Duggan about this privately after this briefing.''

The slide show continued. Each member of individual assault teams, interrogators, police, even medical technicians, was given a separate packet sheet. It was like a massive drug bust without the drugs. Except this was a killer team. Nobody expected any of the targets to submit to arrest. Radios were distributed to all the personnel present. Code names assigned. Weapons checked.

Penelope, looking comically out of place in her miniskirt and heels, was urgently asking Steven Dye for help with her earphone wires, talking a blue streak the whole while.

Michael Barns and Farky were talking earnestly, both hiding essential truths about each team's abilities from the other.

Madeline finally shut off her slide show, set down her pointer, and walked to Steven Dye and Penelope James. She shook Steven's hand and hugged Penelope, causing her to drop her earphone wire for the third time, and then she walked to Con Duggan, her hands reaching for his. Her eyes had the same glittering sparkle he'd noticed earlier. No. Not sparkle. Drugs. That, he knew, was a drug shine. Probably, he thought, from Peter Coy Booker's floating drugstore. He reached into his vest pocket, past the two pistols, and pulled out a long ceramic rose. It was very beautiful. It was also 21A's answer to his request for a tracking device for Maddy. It had a very long, thin stem that served as the means to pin it to her sweater.

"A gift, Maddy. From an admirer."

"You, Con Duggan? Are you an admirer?"

"Yup. Absolutely."

"It's lovely. A bribe, I suppose. To keep me off the bus when you take on the *Stingray*."

"Not my decision, you know."

"No. Not yours. But you know Farky. He must be team leader. To him, that means he tells me what to do. Still, we'll be together at the towers, won't we?"

"Yes. And who knows, you may want to go on a bus ride later."

"Con! You sly devil! I shall wear this lovely flower. Tonight and always." He watched her as she pinned the tracking unit to her sweater. She smiled at him, leaned forward, and kissed his neck. This time, she insinuated her body against his and bit him as well.

"Later, Con. When this is over." The promise in her voice was obvious, and she swayed away, her hips, like Penelope's, waving a sexual message his way. He wondered if there would be a later, and if so, whether she would try to fuck him or kill him. He poured himself a glass of beer and rejoined the U.S. team.

High overhead, Aircraft 21A picked up an activation light on its panel and designated it "Rose One." From now on, as long as she wore the flower, 21A could find Madeline.

From thirty thousand feet, Folkstone was invisible under a fog that reached to five thousand feet before it began to dissipate. But 21A had a thousand electronic eyes and could see as if there were no fog and no dark and no distance. It could also hear.

The U.S. team on the ground was equipped with multipull receivers, and could be guided from target to target from above if required. The British team had no aerial assistance, nor were they aware of it. Con and his team had an edge. They would need it.

Booker had eyes ashore as well, but his eyes had not told him all he needed to know. In a curt phone call to the *Stingray*, he had been informed only that Con Duggan would be taken care of. He had been informed of the arrest of his stewards at the Euro-militaire Exhibition. He'd expected that and had sent only crew members of the boat, men guilty of no more than sailing the *Stingray* from place to place around the world. They were not held. Farky had decided they were more of a nuisance than a menace. Had Booker accompanied his men ashore, he would have been happier, but Farky knew that on the boat, Booker at least presented himself as a target. In his tidy mind, Farky had hoped that the destruction of Booker and his terrorist cell could be accomplished without violence.

But it was not to be. The various terrorist and political extremists, as well as just plain garden-variety thugs, had grown too powerful to deal with any other way. Here, tonight, in foggy, tidy, provincial Folkstone, England, the forces of evil would come face to face with a mirror image of their own methods. With little regard for or worry about the niceties of international civil rights, desperate governments were about to see the black sword of democracy unleashed against terror. It was going to be very messy.

"The Warren" *Folkstone* *11:55 P.M.*

"The Warren," located just east of the first Martello Tower and its three suspected terrorist occupants, was a tangled mass of fauna perfectly suited for a Sherlock Holmes movie starring Basil Rathbone and a hound or two. The fog hung like sticky angel hair, swirling and parting and closing in on Con and Maddy. Con thought it was like trying to acquire a target from inside a jar of milk. He was carrying his oldest and most reliable rifle, the 1903 Springfield 30.06, as well as two pistols, including the massive .500 Linebaugh.

Madeline whispered to Con, though from 400 yards, it was doubtful anyone in or on the Martello Tower would hear them. "We know there are three shooters in there. But we're going to get them to come out if possible."

"How?"

"Ask them."

She nodded at the two British agents accompanying them on the hill, and they picked up a bright yellow bullhorn and headed down to the tower, disappearing in seconds, swallowed by the fog.

"Do you have a plan here, Maddy? What if they don't answer? What if they don't come out?"

"I don't expect them to come out. I *do* expect them to report what is going on to Booker." Her voice was very hard. Even in the darkness, her eyes had an unnatural shine, gathering light from the inside out.

"That may jeopardize Steven and the bus."

"He doesn't know about the bus."

"How do you know that, Maddy?" He made no attempt to hide his doubts. If she was Booker's, he needed to know where she was headed.

"I don't *know* that, Con. But how could he? I didn't know about the gun or the bus until twenty-four hours ago. I don't see any way he could have found out. Do you?"

Below, the bullhorn came to life, blasting through the foggy silence and eliminating the need for Con Duggan to answer Maddy's question.

The demand was put in simple terms. "Put your hands up, and come out peacefully." It was comically insufficient, as Maddy had known it would be.

Aircraft 21A, speaking only to Con Duggan, who was wearing the only wire able to receive 21A information, except for Michael Barns and Steven Dye, knew it as well. They advised him from high above that the men in the tower were contacting Booker, asking what to do. They also advised him that "Rose One," the special bug, was, according to their readout, less than ten feet from him. He acknowledged their information by clicking his receiver twice, the agreed-on signal. He would not speak directly on the secured channel unless absolutely necessary.

"There is no response, Con. I'm going to have a four-man team enter the tower."

"Shouldn't we go down there, Maddy? I don't see what we can do up here in the fog."

"You're right, of course. Well, then, shall we go and see if we can be of assistance?" She grabbed his hand and snapped on a powerful flashlight, providing just enough light to see the trail that wound through the waist-high brush of The Warren. Down below, four muffled explosions went off inside the Martello Tower, one after the other. The terrorists were rolling hand grenades down the interior stairs of the tower. Two of the British Agents were killed as they ascended, the other two were driven back. The clutter of automatic weapons fire ripped through the silence of midnight-bound Folkstone like the tearing of a bedsheet. It seemed to Con Duggan that this was not so much a plan as it was a street fight.

11

The Bus Barn
12:08 A.M.

"Oops! Oh, bloody hell, Steven Yank, what was that!"
Penelope's eyes widened, her mouth framing a perfect
"O" of surprise. Steven Dye had nearly jumped out of
his skin when the explosions had gone off at the Martello
Tower. Penelope James had too, but in a much different
way. Clapping her hands, she ran totteringly about the
garage floor, hopping over weapons and ammo and all
manner of deadly devices as if at a playground. For now,
at least, all this had been play for her.

Steven watched her with dismay. His earphone, both
multichannel and 21A-secured, began to chatter. Orders.
He was getting orders. He listened, his hands pressed to
both ears, as Penelope continued her spinning dance of
excitement around the chilly garage.

"Steven, this is Con. Get the bus down here. We need
some firepower with eyes." Con Duggan's voice
sounded calm, and it calmed Steven Dye as well.

"40mm? Fifty caliber? What?"

151

"Bring all your toys, Steven. I'm going inside with Maddy. Watch your ass and young Penelope's ass too."

"Right! On our way." He was excited, but sure of himself, which came as a considerable shock to him.

"Okay, gang, let's go see it, kill it, and multiply!" He couldn't believe he'd said that. The SIKIM-1000, a joke on Folkstone, England, on a cold foggy night in October 1992. Still, it loosened the four-man team *he* commanded. They burst out laughing and then bent to the task of servicing the most frightening combat system against steel, flesh, and bone ever designed. And he, Steven Dye, had been the force behind its design and birth. Now, tonight, he must make it work.

"Sir, what do we take? What do you need on board the platform?"

Sir, well that was nice. Leadership. They wanted it. Did he have it? Time to find that out as well.

"All modes. Standard .30 caliber, .40 caliber explosive, and .50 caliber anti-materiel. Take plenty of everything."

"Don't forget the enormous dick replacement, Steven darlin'!" Penelope shouted with an obscene wink.

"Right. The EDR and the TAD rounds. Two each. Hopefully, the battery packs, tripled up like I wired them, will allow us to shoot both units, hopefully twice each. But we won't know that until we shoot. Pack the forties and fifties on belts, and tape the clips for the thirties back to back. Penelope, where the hell are you?"

The bus engine roared to life. Penelope yelled out, "All aboard! Zoom, zoom, zoom." The bus lurched forward. She slipped the clutch, and the engine stopped. It burst to life again, and she waved her hand out the window at him.

"Zoom, zoom, zoom, Steven Yank. Onward into the fog! Go shoot them!"

"Sir?"

"Yeah."

"She's right. Why don't we go shoot them?"

"Are you worried about the SIKIM, Robbie?"

"Hell no, sir. I'm just worried we'll get there too late."

He needn't have worried. Folkstone was crowded with people needing to be killed. Zoom zoom, indeed . . .

Con Duggan pressed his back against the cold stone wall of the Martello Tower. In his right hand was the Linebaugh .500. In his right mind, he would have been somewhere else. Next to him, Madeline, also back to the wall, spoke softly into her communication system, trying to raise the agents who had led the way into the tower only to be met by a barrage of grenades.

"Nothing, Con. No reply." She pressed closer to him, and he could feel her breasts against his back. She smelled like bath soap and heat and female pheromones.

"Mr. Duggan?" It was 21A on the secure channel. He clicked twice.

"Rose One is . . . ah, zero distant, sir." Con clicked twice again, then reached for Maddy's hand.

"Let's go in, Maddy. Nothing going on out here." In answer, she squeezed his hand. Pistols ready, they leapt through the open doorway into the dark.

Suddenly, the lower stairway was bathed in light as Madeline swept her flash over the floor, stopping briefly on the shattered, mangled remains of her British comrades. Bits of flesh were stuck to the walls, and the lower third of the stairway was walled in blood. Con could think of nothing to compare it with, except the wash trays of a halibut processor in Alaskan waters. The light swept upward and a hand full of an Uzi automatic appeared around the upper corner of the stairs, and bullets sprayed downward. For a split-second, the gun in hand was visible to Con Duggan. The .500 Linebaugh roared out, and the gun vanished, as the hand holding it took the brunt of 475 grains of lead striking it at 1575 feet per second. The hand ripped free of the wrist, fingers still pressed against the Uzi's trigger, firing even as it sailed out into space and disappeared beyond the circular stairs into the hollow darkness beyond. The hand and the Uzi struck the smooth stone floor, fired twice more, and went silent.

At the top of the stairs, a man's voice screamed in terror, pain, and anguish. The voice was followed by a man's body, one hand clutching the stump of a wrist gushing blood in time to the man's heartbeat. Maddy's light stopped on his chest, and Con Duggan shot one more time. The heavy slug caught the man at the chin, powered upward, and literally tore his head off. The body remained upright, a scene from a color horror movie, then, as if on its own, it walked a few steps and tumbled down the stairway. Con jumped out of the way, but Madeline stood there, rooted to the spot until it crashed into her, carrying her, unhurt but shaken, down the stairs and into what remained of her dead comrades.

She got up, shaking herself like a sleek female wolf placing her Browning 9mm between her body-suited thighs, wiping it clean of blood and guts and bone fragments. Without a word, she pulled herself back up the stone stairway until she was once again at Con's side, the light splashing the upper stairs held firmly, confidently in her hands. Her breasts rose and fell, and he could see her, feel her, smell the battle cry of sweat and dust and fury.

"Nicely done, Mr. Duggan. Thrilling!" Her hand came to rest on his hip, and she urged him on, up the stairs, toward more of the same. Now more than ever, he knew she was a creation of Booker, reveling in blood and violence as a near-sexual release. In spite of his knowledge of what, if not who walked with him, he started up the stairs, no more upset than he'd be at the dentist. Immediately a wholesale volume of automatic weapons opened up on them, spattering the walls with lead and followed by three spheres, black and round and dangerous. They bounced over Con's and Maddy's heads, exploding against the small pieces of flesh left at the bottom of the stairs. Con saw the light.

"Steven, hurry down here."

"On our way, Duggy baby!" It was Penelope. God help them all.

• • •

The bus, driven with considerable verve, if not skill, passed the Leas Cliff headed down the Road of Remembrance, a nostalgic street dedicated to WWI heroes. There was a war memorial atop the road. It was here that the Green Machine, as Penelope called it, began to experience a war of its own. Just below Leas Cliff Hall, the site of Booker's model-making skills, was the "Cliff Lift," built to carry passengers up and down the cliff face. It was a tribute to the ingenuity of its Victorian designers, for it managed to combine efficiency with economy. It was one of England's few remaining water-driven lifts. Water was pumped into the top lift until it became heavier than its counterpart below. The brake was released, and down went the top lift, pulling up the lower lift. And on and on it went. It had been gurgling away happily and safely since 1885.

Now, it was a platform established by Booker to shoot up Leas Cliff Hall and its British agents. He knew they'd been in control of Leas Cliff Hall since 10:00 P.M. He also knew that the harbor exit had been blocked by a "Scalink" British ferry. He could not sail out of Folkstone. So he would shoot his way out.

As it happened, the first counterassault by Booker's onshore force came from the Cliff Lift's, water-filled barrels, populated this night by two armed men firing MB40 Soviet rockets and AK-47 automatic weapons at Leas Cliff Hall, just as the bus nicknamed Green Machine passed by.

"They're shootin' at us, Steven!" Penelope screamed as tracer fire arced out at Leas Cliff from the one-hundred-dred-year-old lift. As it happened, they weren't shooting at the bus. Steven Dye heard Penelope cry out as the bus rocketed along the cobbled "Road of Remembrance."

The SIKIM-1000 was mounted on the second to last seat back on the upper deck. Penelope, directly below him, was trying to drive and direct Steven at the same time.

He had prepared the SIKIM for anti-personnel use at

the Martello Tower. Forty-caliber explosive rounds. He could see the flashes from the upper level of the Cliff Lift, and he could see the glass fronting Leas Cliff Hall exploding under the impact of the AK-47 fire. He swung the barrel of the SIKIM, punched the scope, and got a read on two men. He hit two keys, punched the fire-prep button, and squeezed the trigger. Thirty pounds of .40 caliber high-explosive rounds erupted from the heavy barrel, but the gun remained steady, and the sighting system printed the hits on the interior view scope. Finally, "target down" results registered as the Cliff Lift disintegrated, taking its water barrels and tracks and terrorists down Leas Cliff in a wall of water, wood, flesh, and fire that lit the shoreline with fireworks not seen since the summer festivals. The .40 caliber barrel, hot from firing, glowed and pulsed in the dark.

"Zoom, zoom!" shouted Penelope, gunning the bus past Leas Cliff Hall at fifty miles per hour in the fog, sending the still-hot .40 caliber shell casings rattling off the bus walls and through the glassless windows.

Steven Dye had killed his first bad guys, not to mention an architectural antiquity. From now on, walking would be the only way from Leas Cliff to the seashore.

On the *Stingray*, the only thing Peter Coy Booker knew for sure was that a double-decker bus had just killed two of his best men. He ordered the fifty-caliber shipboard machine-guns loaded and manned. When the fog cleared, he intended to take the bus for a ride.

Con Duggan and Madeline had reached the top of the spiral staircase, under a high volume of fire the whole time. It was not clear where the terrorists had gone, but it seemed a good bet they were outside. On the top of Martello Tower, hiding in the fog, their weapons trained on the roof exit to the broad medieval rampart. The twentieth century attacker/defenders on the roof of Tower #3 had enough firepower between them to slaughter a regiment of Napoleon's troops.

• • •

"Steven, honey, darling, let *me* look!"

Steven Dye was parked thirteen hundred yards from the tower on a bad road above East Cliff Sands. He had the SIKIM-1000 sighting system powered up, and he could "see" them through the fog.

"Let me see!!"

"Shut up, Penelope."

"I want to see!" She sounded like a ten-year-old girl. Acted like one, too.

"Penelope! Shut the fuck up!!"

She looked at him, at her darling Steven Yank, her lover, her savior. His eyes were very cold, angry, father's eyes.

"I'm sorry, Steven," she said in a small, submissive voice, all tone and no substance.

"Good. Now get down behind the plating, and stay out of my way!" Penelope James, for the first time in her relationship with the redheaded man of her dreams, did as she was told.

"Con? I'm ready. I have *five*, repeat, five targets. They are behind fortified positions, although the SIKIM can't tell me what kind. I read you and Madeline, 90, repeat, 90 feet from target. *Do not move*! I'm shooting!"

Before Con could reply, the SIKIM-1000 erupted in a blinding flash of .50 caliber fire, raking the rooftop with 300 belt-fired rounds in 16.5 seconds. The scope read targets down, computed, corrected. One up and moving. Steven Dye hit the fire button one last time. The image-reader in the scope read cool. No hot image.

"Targets down, Mr. Duggan. Target kill confirmed."

"Received, Mr. Dye. My thanks to the SIKIM."

"No sweat, Mr. Duggan." He looked around the bus and saw Penelope looking at him, a look of pure awe tinged with blood lust, and, on a more personal level, straight lust.

"Now, Penelope James, you may look through the scope! The moving figures are on our side. The other, blue-registered figures are dead. . . ."

• • •

The circular top of Martello Tower, even with thick fog swirling and shifting across it, was a scene painted by a surrealist with a thirst for blood. The SIKIM-1000 had ripped across the fortified position and shredded it. The heavy hitting .50 caliber fired from optimum range had done a thorough, if messy, job on the mercenaries so carefully installed to disrupt the official ceremonies. They represented, as did the other shooters still loose in Folkstone, a kind of throw-away force to justify Booker's planned run for cover, safe and richer than ever. It would be thrown away, true. But Peter Coy Booker was anything but safe.

Steven and Penelope jumped off the bus and walked through the fog toward the first Martello Tower to see what the SIKIM had done. Already, Steven Dye had accounted for seven terrorists, although he didn't know the actual count. Fire and debris still flickered dully into the gray-shrouded night where the water lift had smashed down the cliff below the Exhibition Hall. Penelope walked ahead of him, her high heels clacking against the stone road, and in a quirk of nature, he could see her taut buttocks and sleek pale legs through the fog, an apparition both beautiful and torsoless. Penelope began to hurry, a ghostly hand popping briefly through the fog to reach behind her and clasp his.

"Oh, hurry, Steven! Hurry! We must go and see the dead bones. Hurry, Steven!" He didn't know whether her attitude appalled him, amused him, or just plain scared him. Dead bones. Whoopee . . .

"How do you feel about this?" Con Duggan lit a cigarette and handed it to Steven Dye, then lit one for himself.

"I dunno. I never shot up a seaport before, not to mention a Napoleonic tower. It's not much different than the antelope, really. I think I miss the antelope, though."

Steven Dye seemed very calm. More calm than he

should be, or colder than Con had figured? He didn't know.

Madeline was searching by torchlight through what little was left of the sniper team's belongings. The SIKIM had smashed most of their equipment, but it had simply shredded a bulky suitcase. Spread out across the ramparts, what looked to be close to a million dollars was soaking up blood or fog or both.

Steven Dye watched Penelope dart around picking up money, her tight-belted waistband stuffed with bills like a topless dancer's G-string. He walked to her side and turned her around. He realized, and was nearly overwhelmed by, the carnal perfection of this young woman's face. Her eyes, even in the fog, danced and flashed. Innocence amidst the blood and guts of five men she had, in essence, helped him kill.

"No Penelope. Not the money."

"But . . . but Steven, look at it! All you have to do is pick it up. We'll . . . we'll use it properly!"

Steven pulled her closer by her leather-clad hips. The leather was cold and damp, but heat seemed to radiate up from her body and envelop him. He began to pull the bills from her waistband, but she snatched them back and threw her arms around his neck, pulling him tightly against her.

"No, Steven, honey, now we'll keep it, oh, Steven, there's so much money. . . ." She pulled his mouth down to hers, her tongue lashing at his, her hips grinding against him. One high-heeled toe stood on a stack of 100's, while the four-inch heel of the same shoe rested in an inch of blood. In spite of himself, Steven was aroused. Penelope. Oh, poor Penelope. But what else did she know about life? Except the need to survive it. She had, after all, allowed her own mother to sell her "virginity" two hundred times. Briefly, he responded, pulling her tighter against him as she moaned into his ear and whispered endearments, her small fist still tightly closed on a wrinkled pile of bills.

"No, Penelope. We won't do this." He pried her arms

from his neck and the money from her clenched fist. He resumed pulling the money from around her slim waist, astonished by how much there was. She stood quietly, her arms at her sides, her face calm now, her eyes fixed on his.

"I'll take care of you, Penelope James."

"For how long, Steven Yank? For how long?"

"Until you tire of me." He tossed the money to the tower stones and looked at her, still motionless and more composed than he'd seen her before. He could hear his heart thumping against his thin chest.

"I might, you know."

"You might what?"

"Tire of you." She spoke in the voice of the mocking-bird. Their conversation was interrupted by two thunder-ous explosions, and at the entrance to Folkstone Harbor, the Sealink ferry, blocking the harbor entrance to the channel, erupted into two towering red and orange flames, bright enough to shine through the fog.

Penelope turned around and clapped her hands delight-edly. When the machine-gun fire arced across the tower, Steven Dye tackled Penelope and pulled her through the million-dollar goo until they were behind the wall.

"Mr. Duggan, this is 21A." In spite of the turmoil, the voice from above the clouds was loud and clear.

"Go!"

"Booker has, unless our instruments are crazy, torpe-doed the blocking ship. He has also started his engines and is moving slowly *away* from the entrance. Probably worried about residual damage to the *Stingray*. Most likely, if he gets a chance, he's going to boogie out of that harbor."

"Affirmative, 21A. Who is shooting at us?"

"We read a two-man team right there in The Warren with you. Also, Tower Five is preparing to fire mortars."

"Mortars!"

"Life's a bitch, Mr. Duggan. Better be out of there real soon. 'Rose One' is already outside, moving against the two-man team in The Warren. This is a hell of a big operation, Mr. Duggan.''

"Like you said, 21A, life's a bitch.''

Con Duggan then heard a sound he had not heard since Vietnam. The harsh, hiccupping whoosh of mortar fire from Tower Five. He began to realize that if this assault had not been attempted, the landing pad for the chopper carrying the two world leaders was within easy terrorist range. Booker, it seemed, had a better chance to succeed than he'd realized. Better than anybody realized. A rain of mortar fire fell out of the fog and onto the tower.

"Go, go, go! C'mon, outta here!'' Steven Dye was paralyzed, transfixed by the burning Sealink passenger ferry as well as the violent crash of incoming mortars, a sound he'd never encountered. He was immobile. Con Duggan started forward, but he needn't have. Penelope violently pushed Steven toward the circular stairway and comparative safety.

"Come, Steven Yank. I'm not tired of you yet, and you can't bloody well take care of me if you're dead!''

Con had no idea what she was talking about, but they cleared the tower safely. Another of the British agents wasn't so lucky, and a mortar burst right on top of him, adding to and rearranging the mess on the tower top.

To Steven Dye, this was the worst moment of the mission. Huddled in the fog, crawling on his belly toward an invisible pair of Palestinian mercenaries trying to kill him while all around him mortars exploded. Occasionally, the earth erupted near him, miraculously not killing him, and clearing the fog away as well.

Ahead of Con, only yards away, Madeline crawled on her belly, arms outstretched, a Belgian FN assault rifle cradled across her wrists. Con was too old to crawl around behind a young female agent he thought might later try to kill him.

He jumped up and sprinted forward, the .500 Linebaugh and a .44 Desert Eagle blazing away at nothing. It made him feel better. A mortar round went off nearby, and Madeline cried out. But not in pain. More in triumph. The fog swept away, swirling up as if pulled on a rope, and the two men were right there, only ten yards away, up and running away. Con should have shot them, but before he could, he realized Madeline had leapt on the back of one of them, knocking him to the ground. As he raced after the other one, he heard a gurgling, strangled cry, and glanced down in time to see Maddy stick a slim, long-bladed knife into the man's throat. After that, he was in a fight of his own.

Con had not seen the kick that knocked him onto his back, his breath expelled, his chest a hot pain. He tried to get up, was knocked down again, this time by the man's hand. The man faced him, a swarthy face, mustached, bearded, and completely unafraid. The harbor lit up again as a third explosion lifted the Sealink ferry and smashed it into two sections, drifting apart as they burned. He was struck again, this time by a whirling, spinning assailant who grunted with each blow. The man pulled back, dancing, as Con tried to shake off the pain and wooziness. He was in good shape, but his assailant had more weapons. Well, almost more.

Con pulled the twenty-year-old A. G. Russell boot knife he had carried for almost half his adult life, and the next time the man advanced, Con stepped forward under the flying leg and buried it in the man's groin. Then he ripped down and stepped away. The man looked at him, but did not scream. He was trying to push his guts back where they belonged when he pitched forward flat on his face and died.

Con stuck the knife back into his boot, picked up both his pistols, and turned around to help Maddy. She stood there, the FN assault rifle in the crook of her arm, smoking a cigarette.

"Why didn't you shoot him, Maddy? He was about to kill me."

"Oh, but he didn't kill you, did he? Come, Mr. Duggan, let's get out of here and deal with the next tower, shall we?"

"Why didn't you shoot him?" Con wanted to know,

and if the answer didn't fit, he would have no more doubts.

"Frankly, it didn't occur to me. I was sure you'd be just fine. Shall we go on?"

No kiss this time. She just walked away into the night.

There was general gunfire throughout Folkstone now, as a mission not very well planned because of time limits degenerated into personal, brutal firefights. The citizens of Folkstone had temporarily joined in the battle. When the Sealink ship blew up, scores of fishing boats and private yachts burst into flame, one after another. The citizens, drawn to the flames like moths, quickly discovered a blocking force of policemen and soldiers that seemed to rise from the fog like magic. Folkstone is not very big, and a quarter of its harbor was ablaze. Three onlookers were killed at the waterlift and six more on the harbor. The rest of Folkstone allowed themselves to be herded away, back into the officially ordered blackout, a sight even the older citizens had not seen in nearly fifty years.

Martello Tower Number Five, the source of the mortar and machine-gun fire, was to be handled by Con and Michael Barns. Con would shoot, Michael would spot for him. Madeline would, for now, just watch. There was a sniper's area above the tower, a flat area with a sharply dropped edge. It was, in fact, a cricket field, and it was nine hundred yards from the tower. Like the whole action, this shoot would be fairly spontaneous. The SIKIM-1000 would kick them out, and Con would kill them.

Peter Coy Booker was racing toward the blazing hulk of the ferry, now split in two pieces and drifting farther and farther apart. He poked the nose of the fast moving Zodiac boat into the gap, and head down, powered through it and out into the English Channel. Only blackness and the sea stretched before him. In the distance, he could see a row of lights, then another. Coastal patrol boats. He was not yet safe, but they would be too slow and too timid to stop him. The *Stingray* had a top speed of 44 knots, and the channel was calm. He turned back and slipped into the wreckage once more. Back in the Folkstone Harbor, he had seen for himself the success of the torpedo's work. He had a clear, if not straight, course to open water.

Aboard the bus and below the cricket field, Penelope James had lurched off Cheriton Road and then driven into and through the Central Railway Station. Tower Number Five was in a completely open area, near St. Steven's Way and Coolinge Lane. Soft names for hard times. As Penelope headed down Goodwyn Road, the bus began to shudder as it took rifle fire from the tower.

"Penelope, get us out of here. Take us somewhere close, but somewhere we might not get dead!" As bullets zipped around inside the bus, Penelope, twisting in her driver's seat, jammed the old Green Machine into reverse and backed up the street, bouncing across curbs and bushes and lawns, ricocheting off cars and homes and the brightly canopied carts of commerce used in this touristy city. She remained in reverse for 1200 yards, not road, and she did over $120,000 damage to Folkstone in the process. Finally, the bus came to a jarring halt, and she jumped almost directly from the seat into Steven's arms. She gave him a resounding kiss, so resounding he tripped and fell to the bus deck, Penelope on top of him.

"We're safe now, Steven Yank. They can't kill us here. But you can shoot them to a fair-thee-well!"

"Where are we, Penelope?"

"We're protected, Steven. Lots of things to hide behind. This old bus will live to drive again!"

"Penelope, *where are we?*" It was pitch dark outside the bus.

"The cemetery. We're in the bloomin' Folkstone cemetery. No threat here, Steven Yank! Everybody here is already dead!"

• • •

Con Duggan looked at his watch, startled to see it had been only 46 minutes since the first shot had been fired. So much blood, so much violence, so little time for men to die. Now, spread out below him, the harbor burned, the shoreline burned, Folkstone was a city under assault. Who, exactly, were the good guys? He didn't know. He didn't care.

"Mr. Duggan?"

"Roger, 21A."

"Booker has tested the harbor entrance. It is our belief he will attempt a breakout as soon as he can."

"Roger, 21A."

"Mr. Duggan?"

"Go."

"Rose One is stationary at a distance of 8.3 feet."

"Roger, 21A. I see Rose One."

Maddy had propped herself against the bleachers at the cricket field, the FN assault rifle slung over her shoulder. She had a pair of binoculars held to her face focused on Martello Tower Number Five. She looked beautiful in spite of the mayhem she had been involved in. She ran on a drug clock, of course. She would be "up" until this was all over. She looked away from the binoculars and straight at Con Duggan. Her eyes had no expression, none at all. She smiled. Her mouth smiled, but her eyes told him the same old story: Watch your back.

"Con, where the hell is Mr. Dye? We need him to shoot that place up. Tell him I want him to knock the place down from the bottom up. I want the bad guys either outside running or on top."

"You got right back into this, huh, Michael?"

"Yup. Truth told, I'm having a good time. And I'm sure Booker's plan would have succeeded, to what degree I'm not sure, but these guys would have put out a whole lot of hurt."

"I think you're right, Michael. We turned out to be the cavalry after all." Then Duggan keyed Steven Dye. "Steven, where are you?"

"Right below you, Con. In the graveyard."

"That figures. Penelope's idea?"

"She's the driver. Besides, she was right. I can tear that place up from here if you want me to."

"I want. Forty millimeter explosive. You have to drive them out or upstairs."

"When?"

"Now, Mr. Dye. Right now."

The EDR and the TAD round, when used in the SIKIM-1000, were awesome, but mostly because of what they did and the exotic way they did it. The .40mm explosive rounds were destructive, loud, and terrifying. The SIKIM dealt them out at 120 rounds a minute, one every half-second.

Penelope, a bright learner, had picked up very quickly how to help Steven Dye. Keep the gun loaded. He showed her how, and she never missed a beat. When Steven looked through the SIKIM-1000 sighting system, he got no readout and no individual targets. Like Joshua at the gates, he just tried to blow the wall down.

The tower looked to Steven like a fat, old-fashioned milk bottle made out of stone from another century. The 21st century SIKIM-1000 could not exactly blow it up, but it could chip at it until the men inside lost their nerve or their minds. He settled in behind the gun and grew very calm. The SIKIM always made him calm. He touched the prep button, and the scope began to throb with light, outlining the tower. He centered the massive scope with its readout and computer systems on the rectangular-shaped entrance. He slipped the switch to fire, and the SIKIM-1000 went about the business of chasing the sniper team with mortar capabilities into Con Duggan's .30 caliber relic. The gun began to spit out .40 caliber explosive rounds, bucking and belching fire, a slender rapid-fire Howitzer from the upper deck of a shot-up old bus parked in a graveyard.

"Jesus, Con, look at that son-of-a-bitch!"

"Yeah, it's a wonderful gun, all right."

"Con, I shall have to report to Reggie Farquarson at the police center after we deal with the tower. We must decide what to do to get Booker." Maddy had moved to his side, a faintly curious look on her face as she studied his old beat-up .03.

"Doesn't look like much," she said. "A bit haggard, isn't it, Con?"

"Yeah. Me and the gun. Both old, both haggard. Still, it will do."

"I'm sure it will in your capable hands. How can I assist you, Con?"

"You can spot with me if you like. Michael will find them, though, if they pop out."

"Well, fine then, all looks under control here. I shall just skip down to see Reggie. Perhaps we'll go after Booker straight away. With Farky, one never knows." Maddy drew herself up, and in the brief respite between actions in Folkstone, she bent forward and kissed the back of his neck. A very cool, cold-lipped kiss. Then she was gone into the night, taking her two remaining team members from British Intelligence with her.

Con and Michael Barns were alone on the cricket field, while below them, the bus flashed and lit up like a party of cameramen gone mad had been set loose aboard it. Con reminded himself, as the SIKIM continued its steady assault on the tower, to address the problem when they got back to the States. In the dark at full auto or like now, at a steady two rounds a second, the SIKIM lit the bus up like a Roman candle. The dark green silhouette stood out clearly in the light. It wouldn't be long before it drew more fire from the *Stingray*, particularly if the boat tried to escape the harbor, which would actually bring it closer to the cemetery position.

"Mr. Duggan?"

"Go ahead, 21A." Clear as a bell, the angel voice from the sky whispered in his ear. "Rose One is now two hundred yards away and has entered the police station."

"Thanks, 21A."

"No problem, Mr. Duggan. The *Stingray* is powered

up and moving. The whole town is on fire down there. Lots of fire from up here. Looks like London in the blitz.''

"Thanks, 21A, and keep tabs on Rose One. We should be running out of bad guys down here soon.''

"Roger, Mr. Duggan. The Brits have silenced all other opposition in Folkstone proper. Cold feet, I guess. There were seventeen more of them!''

"Good thing they quit, 21A.''

"Roger, Mr. Duggan. We'll keep you posted. 21A out.''

At that moment, Michael Barns tugged Con back to the business at hand. "Con, two on the tower top and two going over the side on ropes. Can you pick 'em out?''

Con bent forward, snatched the sniper rifle to his shoulder, and cinched the sling straps. Just like old times. He sat down on the cricket field grass and brought the night-capable scope to his eyes. He could see very clearly, though the fire in the background silhouetting the Martello Tower slightly distorted his targets. It was time to turn off the SIKIM.

"Mr. Dye?''

"Yah, Con, I'm still getting no sure readout, but I'll keep up the pressure. Hell, it might fall over.''

Con chuckled into his mouthpiece. In the background, he could hear Penelope screaming, "Shoot, shoot, shoot, shoot!'' at the top of her considerable lungs.

"I have them, Mr. Dye. Shut down. I'll take them from here.''

The SIKIM went silent.

Meanwhile in the police station, Maddy asked for permission to remain with Con Duggan for the final assault on the *Stingray*. Distracted, Reggie Farquarson waved her out the door. On the way out, she presented the only other female agent on the British strike force with a beautiful, long stemmed, porcelain rose, then she slipped off into the dark, her eyes glittering, wet with anticipation. It would soon be time to take the SIKIM-1000 for herself.

• • •

Con balanced the '03 Springfield over his knees in a sitting position. He was an old dog, perfect for old-dog tricks.

"Get the one on the rope first. The other two are stationary now. They must be pretty shook up." Michael sounded very calm and very sure of what he was saying.

Con centered the rifle on the target dangling from the end of a too short rope. He was too high to jump, and Con thought he could hear him crying out to his mates for help as he struggled to climb back up the rope. Folkstone had gone still, the quiet before the final storm. Con did not think. Experience simply guided him through the mechanics of killing a man in the dark, far away and unaware he was about to be killed. The rifle kicked, a solid, reassuring thump as he chambered another round, found the two men on the roof, fired again, chambered, switched targets, fired again, and stood up.

"Con? I still get no reading!" Steven was speaking low but urgently into Con's half-blocked-out consciousness. The sniper's blanket.

"You get no reading, Mr. Dye, because the team in the tower is accounted for. Thanks for the assist. I'll be down soon to direct the operation against the *Stingray*."

"Okay, Con. We'll be here. Us and the tombstones."

"21A?"

"Yes, Mr. Duggan?" It had ceased to amaze him that he was speaking to a man flying five miles over his head.

"Scratch the tower. We'll be shifting soon to take the *Stingray*."

"You're a little late, Mr. Duggan. *Stingray* is up and running. She's making a break for the sea."

"Where is Rose One, 21A?"

"Still at the police station, Mr. Duggan. She's beaping steady, loud, and clear."

"Okay. Keep me informed at all times about Rose One."

"Okay, Mr. Duggan. Don't you worry. Oops! Guns up on the *Stingray*."

Con looked out into the harbor, bright with hot fire and burning fuel oil. From one end of her sleek hull to the other, as she sped toward the hole left by the burning Sealink ferry, the *Stingray* began to spit out a torrent of machine-gun fire. Every third round was a tracer, and the rounds arced out across the beach and began to shoot up the bus. Booker had finally located the main source of all his grief ashore, as well as the only likely deterrent to his escape. Long necklaces of light began to walk their way through the graveyard as the *Stingray* raced toward freedom.

"Mr. Dye. You will have to take him. I can't help you from here." Con felt the tension in Steven's voice. The answer was direct.

"I got him!"

Aboard the *Stingray* as it picked up speed, Peter Coy Booker looked about him with satisfaction from the bridge. He was going to make it. He always made it. Below him, gunfire from the *Stingray* continued to pour out, racking Folkstone Cemetery and the area around it. He had lost contact with his people ashore, but it didn't matter. The *Stingray* picked its way through the wreckage of the harbor 200 yards from the channel.

"Penelope! I'm going to shoot at the *Stingray!* Get the TAD round and the barrel for it out of that gray bag!" He didn't have to tell her twice. She scrambled around the deck as lead smacked against the old bus like a thousand heavy stones. The bus shuddered, and the remaining glass shattered. Light everywhere. Something whispered by his cheek, something else slipped through his leather jacket, the tug of an impatient lead child, anxious to be on its way. A thin but not fatal line of blood, no worse than a paper cut, marked its passage across his chest.

He began to return fire, this time full auto, and the tough little .40mm began to slap against the *Stingray*. He sprayed the lower decks, left to right, right to left, chewing and chipping up everything above the waterline. The boat was clear in his sighting system, alive with targets. He kept the trigger depressed until the boat shuddered to a halt, its engine running, but its rudder shot away. The *Stingray* began to go around in circles, its decks a shambles of downed men and silent guns. Steven could see one man clearly, standing in a shattered window, manning what seemed to be the last operational machine-gun.

"Penelope?"

"Right here, Steven Yank."

"Hand me that barrel and the tool that's strapped to it. And get me the red dildo this time."

"Oh, yes, the red dildo. It's *bigger* than the enormous dick replacement!"

"Hotter, too."

Calmly but speedily, Steven Dye removed the hot .40mm barrel and tossed it clattering across the bus floor. He snapped the larger, much heavier TAD barrel on in seconds. TAD . . . Thermal Accelleration Device. Half the time it didn't work.

Steven could feel Penelope's shoulder against his as he inserted the heavy TAD round into the breech of the new barrel and powered up the scope for a TAD-shot readout. He glanced at Penelope, but she paid him no attention, her eyes fixed on the *Stingray* as it circled helplessly in the harbor. Every time it got into position, the one machine-gun would open up again, lead singing through the cemetery and blasting the bus, miraculously turning it to junk without killing them.

The *Stingray* readout clicked through the shot computer in 14.5 seconds, printed its data, and held. The scope went blue, and the heat from the gun on the boat and its one-man crew pulsed a steady yellow light, shifting numbers to the side as the boat circled.

Steven Dye was positive the lone gunman on the bridge was Peter Coy Booker. The scope readout locked on the *Stingray*, selecting an aim point automatically. The scope face turned red, and a green-colored range and speed printed a series of numbers from 2800 yards to 2841 yards. Steven switched on the pack, transferring the selection bar from ready to fire optimum, FO on the receiver switch panel, which contained two other switches: FM for fire manual and SS for sightless shot, meaning no scope. In the fire optimum mode, the scope, in effect, did the shooting. For him, at the most perfect time, the TAD whooshed away at the optimum selected range of 2870 yards. It struck the *Stingray* directly amidships under Booker and his gun. It struck the section of the *Stingray* made almost exclusively of wood. A fire of awesome proportions erupted along the full length of the *Stingray*, and then as it met an onrushing plume of vapor from a ruptured fuel tank, the *Stingray* seemed to vanish inside a white-hot ball of flame. In less than 15 seconds, it was gone without a flicker. From 21A, circling 25,000 feet overhead, someone said, ''Holy Shit!''

Con glassed the harbor for a trace of the *Stingray*, but he couldn't find one. The TAD round, unpredictable most of the time, had applied more heat in one small place than any other weapon ever developed. They had done it. Peter Coy Booker was dead.

''21A?''

''Yeah, Mr. Duggan.''

''Where is Rose One?''

''Still in the station, Mr. Duggan.''

''Good. You can set her down now. We'll let the Brits clean up the mess. Michael says we're going home.''

''All right! 21A out.''

''We did it, didn't we, Steven Yank?''

''Yup. We did it. Nobody got out of that. The damn gun really surprised me.''

''Oh, why?''

''It worked, that's why. I wasn't sure it would.''

Penelope walked around the bus, but hopped would be a more apt description. A machine-gun slug had shot off one of her high heels.

''Oh, Steven, it will never *zoom-zoom* again.'' She sounded genuinely sad as she walked to him.

"Now, Steven Yank, you must honor your promise and take me with you to the United States."

"Did I promise that? When? When did I say that?" His face was blackened like a coal miner's from powder residue. He pulled her to him until she wiped the grin off his face by trying to swallow his tongue with her own.

"How sweet. I hate to break this up, but I'm taking the weapon. Unfortunately, I can't allow you to live." Madeline stood in what was left of the bus's doorway, gun in hand.

Penelope broke free from Steven, tripping on her heelless shoe, falling down.

21A had been only half right. Rose One, the listening device, was still in the police station, but the wrong agent was wearing it. Maddy raised the Browning .9mm and pointed it at Steven Dye.

"I would like to have fucked you both before you left for the States. Now, of course, you won't be leaving. Stand clear of the gun."

Nine hundred yards away, Con Duggan could hear everything Maddy said. Steven Dye's communicator was open. He had neglected to close it during the battle with the *Stingray*.

Con centered the Springfield's cross-hairs on Madeline, who was standing erect and starkly outlined, her gun hand extended toward Steven Dye. He could see her sleek shape, so feminine and yet so dangerous. As he slowly tightened his finger on the trigger, the figure in the cross-hairs wavered, fogged, reappeared, this time holding a child, not a gun. Sweat beaded his forehead, his mouth dry and tasting of rust and forests and blood. The figure in the scope wavered back and forth from a woman with a gun to a woman seeming to hold a child. The next time the figure appeared to hold a gun, he ended the Folkstone contract by sending a 200-grain Columbia bullet, identical to the last one he'd fired in Southeast Asia, roaring out across the cemetery and crashing into Maddy's brain. His scope was empty. His ghosts were buried.

Highgate Hempstead Surgical Hospital
London, England
December 15, 1992

Mr. Smith walked slowly down the semidarkened hallway of the private hospital supported at the arms by two
burly men in heavy coats. He had refused to sit in the
wheelchair, his voice gruff and hoarse. The head nurse
thought Mr. Smith had a Welsh accent, but she couldn't
be sure. His face was covered by a low, brimless hat, and
a silk scarf was thrown loosely around his neck. She had
seen only the fire of his eyes caught in the light of her
night desk lamp. There had been something very odd
about his eyes. She wasn't sure what it was. Only later
would she recall that he'd had no eyebrows.

Dr. Malcolm Keeler was considered by his peers to be
one of the finest reconstructive surgeons in the United
Kingdom. He was 54 years old, the son of a surgeon and
the grandson of another. He lived in a mansion near
Richmond Park, where he regularly rode his thorough-

bred Arabian horse with his second cousin Gwen, who happened to be a duchess. He was a bit of a playboy, though happily married to the same woman for thirty years. He had a collection of flashy cars and flashier young women. He never drove the cars. He did drive the women. He was that most odd of famous people, the medical-genius celebrity. He was often featured in magazines read by the poor but dedicated to the rich. He was strikingly handsome, with deep-set blue eyes, a patrician face, and a shock of stark white wavy hair that somehow made him look younger than he was. He did not practice at this small private hospital north of London, but he had been called in to consult and give his expert opinion. All he knew was that his patient had been injured and burned in a boating accident. At first he had declined, saying he had neither the time nor the inclination to do such work. He was happier tucking tummies and enlarging breasts. Then the director of Highgate Hempstead Surgical Hospital had said the magic words. One million pounds. Cash. The good doctor was undoubtedly a snob. But he was no fool.

Now Doctor Keeler was seeing his new patient for the first time. He couldn't see the two men standing silently in the corners of the examining room. The room was unlit except for the strong lights shining directly down on Mr. Smith, who was dressed in black pajamas with a flaming dragon on the pocket, an image made no less savage by the delicate embroidery work that had taken fifty hours to complete. Mr. Smith's face was gently wrapped in gauze bandages. Only his eyes and mouth were visible.

"Tell me, Doctor, is it possible to change a man's face so that nobody he ever knew or met would recognize him?"

"That depends, Mr. Smith."

"On what?"

"What the surgeon has to work with. I've not examined you, but I've been told by the staff here that you have suffered very serious burns as well as some bone breakage. Without examining you personally, I can't give you a proper diagnosis.''

"Right then, I can bloody well see that. Why don't you look for yourself, Doctor?''

"This will be very painful, Mr. Smith. I must probe a bit, most likely.''

"Get on wi' it, mate. I don't bloody much care about the pain. I want to remember it. It keeps my mind on the future. Go ahead then.''

The doctor stepped forward, his nostrils assailed by the antiseptic smell of ointments and tape and rebuilding tissue. He wrinkled his nose in distaste. He'd done only cosmetic reconstruction on the wealthy for the past decade. Not since the Falklands War had he dealt with burned and broken bodies. He'd done some quite marvelous work back then. Some of those brave young chaps had practically no face at all when he started on them. He felt a little unexpected thrill of discovery, of anticipation. He was, after all, a healer, not just a creator of firm breasts and taut cheek, both facial and posterior.

He was very careful removing the bandages, but Mr. Smith tensed each time he looped another layer around his head. But he did not cry out. Perhaps it was not as bad as he'd been told. But as the last bandages came free, he saw that it was worse. Much worse.

Mr. Smith had no face whatever. It was as if a hot hand had swept across the flesh and burned it to the bone. The flesh was taut, the bright red of new skin prodding and pushing at the charred remains of the old. The cheekbones were smashed, the jaw broken, reset, and needing to be broken and reset once, possibly twice more. Mr. Smith looked like a garishly painted, greased up laboratory cadaver. *He had no face*. On the other hand, he was essentially a blank slate.

Dr. Malcolm Keeler probed and poked at what he now viewed as a flat human canvas waiting for his skilled hands and artist's mind to bring to life again. The fire, or whatever it was, had damaged only the face. The neck and shoulders were unscarred. There was a small surgical scar on the right shoulder. A bullet wound, he knew. Clearly, Mr. Smith had suffered more than an "accident." He fixed his gaze on the man's eyes. They were the eyes of a fanatic, glistening with fierce desire or hate or who knew what. They were not the eyes of a sane man.

"I've seen worse, Mr. Smith. Not much worse—but worse. I can give you a new face. It will *have* to be a new face, because the one you've got left will be of no help at all. I shall have to change your bone structure, your cheeks, chin, forehead. You will be whole, but no one will ever know who you were before, because you'll not look even a whit like you used to look."

"How much, including my hand?"

"Your hand?"

Mr. Smith extended his left arm. It too was wrapped in gauze bandages.

"I didn't know you'd injured your arm as well."

"It's burned and twisted. The other docs say it'll heal up but stay ugly, and my fingers will keep lookin' like bloody talons on a bloody eagle. Do you agree? And if so, what do you suggest?"

The doctor unwrapped the arm, looked at it briefly, and rewrapped it. "The others were right, and so are you. It does look more like a talon than a man's hand. It is healing, if you call that healing. Your fingers will never straighten out. I suggest you have an amputation, if you simply don't want to look at it, or have it looked at. Or I can do some work on it, straighten it a bit, and you can wear a leather glove over it."

"What then? A bloody mangled hand, or no hand at all, or a leather hand, that's bloody it?"

"You will never be able to use that hand in any case. It will, I'm afraid, simply be there on the end of your arm. Your hand will be of no use to you. That is my opinion."

Mr. Smith gave him a very curious look, his eyes the only thing of life left to his destroyed face.

"Leather hand, huh? I like that, Doc. I really do. I'll find something to do with it. I'll find uses for my leather hand you'd never bloody imagine." The mouth that was

just a gaping hole amid the wreckage did its best to smile.
A ghoul's smile.

"All right then. That's decided. Now about the costs
involved here, Mr. Smith."

"The cost doesn't matter. Results matter. Can you give
me a face I can use or not?"

"Well, you won't be handsome, perhaps. But I can
give you a very respectable face, yes."

"Time. Time is important. How much time are we
talking about?"

"First, you must heal up, not in the truest sense, but
healed enough to work on. Skin grafts. Many of them.
Bone breakage and replacement. Then, and only then,
can I actually construct a brand new face."

"How much time?" The voice was a hiss, a curled
snake, impatient to strike.

"One year. Perhaps two. I'm not sure. It will depend
to some extent on much how pain you can stand."

"I can stand whatever pain you've got, Doctor. One
year. No more. Do it in one year, and I'll give you a
million-dollar bonus."

"It's not the money, Mr. Smith. I'm a doctor, not a
magician. I won't rush this, even for a million dollars."

"Sure, it's the money, Doctor. You don't even know
who I am. And you won't, either. One year and a half
then. Is it a bloody deal or not?"

"I'll let you know." Malcolm Keeler turned away,
gathering his coat and hat. The hiss voice brought him up
short.

"That suitcase over there contains half a million dollars, unmarked cash. Decide now or walk away."

The doctor looked at the suitcase and back at the apparition he was being asked to turn back into an identifiable human being. The eyes, deep in their sockets, flared
and burned out at him, brighter than he thought possible.
Optical illusion, perhaps. He suddenly realized he had no
freedom of choice. A chill swept his body, and death
watched him pick up the suitcase and start for the door.
He stopped and gave his patient a hard look. "We start

on Monday, Mr. Smith. And it won't be pleasant. On that note, I bid you goodnight."

His patient remained seated and silent.

The White Cork Bar
London, England
December 24, 1993

The girl was very beautiful and very lonely. It was Christmas Eve, and she wore a shimmering green dress, scooped low in front, exposing creamy, full breasts that bounced unconfined at her every movement. Damn Johnny Roberts! Who did he think he was, taking her to the office Christmas party and then leaving with that blowsey Doreen creature, the skinny bitch from the accounting section! It was true what they said. Sleep with Johnny, and he'll treat you like some whore, only worse!

She was working on her fifth whiskey and she was getting very drunk. The White Cork Bar was full of couples, but the few single men in the place were either too old, too fat, or worse: not interested in her. The woman of their dreams. Faggots, most likely. She spilled a bit of whiskey, dabbing after it, down between her breasts, her fingers wet with whiskey after the first plunge. She spilled the rest of the glass in her lap and burst into tears of frustration.

"Allow me, miss. Please, take this." A silk handkerchief appeared as if by magic, the hand very slim and the nails manicured. A large diamond solitaire decorated the man's little finger. A *very* large diamond. She took the rescuer's proffered handkerchief and dabbed at her eyes.

"May I join you?"

She looked up, a smile of gratitude and interest on her face. The first thing she saw was his eyes. So *bright*. So . . . odd. His face was quite handsome in the way you would expect a model's face to be. A full mouth over good teeth, high pronounced cheekbones that made her think of a painting she'd once seen of an American Indian chief. His skin was very pale, without a wrinkle. He looked to be about thirty, but he had pure white hair. He looked perfect. Unnaturally so. On the handkerchief were the initials M.B.

"Let me introduce myself. My name is Martin Brooks. I'm British, from Canada by way of Hong Kong. And why, may I ask, is a girl as beautiful as you are sitting alone in this bar on Christmas Eve?"

"Thank you. Yer a real gentleman. I'm waiting for my boyfren, but I'm getting tipsier by the glass. Whiskey does that. Makes me cry, too. He wouldn't be late, normally, but . . . but I think he's . . . drunk somewhere! That's it! Drunk. So I'm alone, and I'd be happy if you'd join me." She hiccupped and lifted her hand to her mouth, smiling at him. A charming, sexy little drunk, all by herself in a dress two sizes too tight for her body.

"Would you like to switch to something more festive? Champagne, perhaps?" He had a cultured voice, a bit raspy, but sexy. He had no identifiable British accent. Just a vague something. He sounded like a voice over a radio commercial for expensive motor cars.

"I'm Karen. Karen Black. I work at Harrod's."

"You must be one of their best sales persons."

"Me? Sales? Thanks, but not likely! I work in the dungeon. Accounting. We call that department the dungeon. I could never work the floor. God, I'd hate to deal with all those hoity toity snotty bitches from Kensington and such places! I mean, I can see you're a perfect gentleman and all, and I mean nothing by it. It's just rich women are so awfully pushy, I think."

"Oh, I quite agree. The rich can be awfully pushy." He motioned to the waiter and ordered champagne. It was then she saw the leather-gloved hand. The fingers were bent only at the tips, slightly downward. They did not seem to move.

He noticed her glance. "Yachting accident. Boat caught fire. My wife and children were aboard. I tried to get back aboard after being thrown into the water. No luck. Burned my hand, and the boat sank."

"How awful. Wot about your family?"

"Gone, I'm afraid. I'm a widower."

Well, Karen Black thought, there must be a Santa Claus after all. She leaned forward and took his "hand" in hers. Her dress fell away from her body, a sequinned veil barely covering her nipples.

"We're both alone then, Mr. Brooks."

"So it would seem. Please, call me Martin." He looked straight down the front of her dress, then back at her face.

His eyes! She had never seen eyes that bright. She pulled her shoulders forward a bit more. Her breasts were now completely visible. He looked down again and smiled.

"Shall we take our leave of this tawdry little bar? I'm at the Ritz Carlton. We could celebrate Christmas there." His good hand reached into his breast pocket and pulled out a hotel key.

"I'm, well, I mean, we don't hardly know each other."

"What better way then? Come, Karen Black, let's go see what Santa has for you."

It seemed she had no will of her own. She got up and went with him. Outside, it had begun to snow. A sleek silver limousine sat at the curb. A wiry Asian in a dark blue suit held the door open for them.

"This is yours? My god, Mr. Brooks!" She clapped her hands and nearly fell over.

"Martin. Please call me Martin."

"Oh, yeah, Martin. Well, let's go!" Like a delighted child, she climbed into the huge rear seat of the limo. The partition between the front seat and the rear slid shut. He wasted no time, simply pulling her to him, his leather-gloved hand grabbing the front of her dress and jerking downward, ripping it clear of her body. Her panties were jerked down almost as quickly.

"Hey! Hey, wait a minute, what are you trying to do? Hey, wait. . . ."

But he didn't wait, and before she could stop him, her legs were spread wide. She tried to resist, to cry out, but he rammed in and out of her with such power and force she found herself biting at his suited shoulder and cursing at him. He only laughed.

"I *know* women like you. I have *always* known women like you!" When he was through with her, she curled up in the corner, crying, ashamed, but unhurt. A packet of hundred-dollar bills bounced off her naked hip and onto the floor.

"Pick it up, Karen Black. Your life has just begun." He stroked her naked thighs, his hand, the leather hand, inserting itself between her thighs. She gasped out loud, but did not move away.

The glass partition slid open at the touch of a button.

"Yes, sir?"

"It all seems to work, Chin."

"Yes, sir."

The glass slid shut again. Martin Brooks, aka Peter Coy Booker, had a new face, a new accent, and the beginning of a new team of helpers. The operations were a success. The patient, all things considered, had already been dead. Now he had only one thought in mind. The violent death of Con Duggan . . .